Gravier's Bookshop
A New Orleans Paranormal Mystery

by
Evelyn Klebert

Gravier's Bookshop
A New Orleans Paranormal Mystery
By Evelyn Klebert

A Cornerstone Book
Published by Cornerstone Book Publishers

First Cornerstone edition 2013
Second Cornerstone edition 2019
Third Cornerstone edition 2023
Fourth Cornerstone edition 2026

Cornerstone Book Publishers
Hot Springs Village, AR
www.cornerstonepublishers.com

ISBN 978-1-61342-288-5

Dedication

For Michael,
My Knight, My Inspiration, My Forever

Table of Contents

Gravier's Bookshop
A New Orleans Paranormal Mystery

THE LIBRARY

1

The sky had darkened to the extent that, at any moment, one could expect a downpour. There was only enough time to decide whether or not to indulge the peculiar impulse plaguing him all morning or to simply let it go. So, he did what he always did. Following his instincts, he took a deep breath and opened his car door. Slamming it abruptly behind him, he tore up the Milton Latter Library steps just as the raindrops began to hit the outside of his sports coat. As he pushed the heavy doors aside that felt nearly icy in his hands, he watched the deluge of rain come down just outside. His heart was pumping wildly, and he considered as an afterthought that perhaps it would have been expedient to grab the small compact umbrella he stored beneath the passenger's seat of his Jeep. But shrugging off that notion, he walked into the cold foyer of the library.

The structure used to be the house, more aptly called the mansion, of a former silent movie star. It was one of the palatial buildings, and there were many, along New Orleans' famous St. Charles Avenue. It had been years since he'd been here, and in many ways, he found it odd that he was here today. But last night had been plagued with dreams of this place, dreams of this place, and a young woman with long chestnut-colored hair. So, he'd closed the bookstore he owned on Magazine Street early this morning—one of the perks of being the owner—and set off on this peculiar quest to unravel the meaning of his dream. For dreams, as his very astute grandmother had once told him, were something not to be ignored.

The inside of the library was largely silent, which made his entrance all the more noticeable or, rather, would have been if anyone was around. He paused at the door, his eyes taking in the vast stretch of mildly wearing mosaic floor. This definitely had been a home once—someone's home, only now a bit unnaturally converted into this public building. The lingering of lives passed here long ago clung profoundly to the place, layers of impressions—the past clearly more powerful and dominant than the present.

He focused deeply, trying to filter out the impressions that were non-essential to him from those he sought. His lightweight canvas tennis shoes hit the highly polished floor but were largely silent, fortunately.

Again, he focused on the dream—the young woman, green-eyed, with long reddish-brown hair. His feelings stretched out. Maximilian, or Max as he preferred, was a closet psychic.

◆

It was inexplicable the wash of despair that had flooded over her this morning, just pure cascades of desolation. Caroline had wandered around her Carrolton Avenue apartment aimlessly, her head nearly splitting open with a migraine incited by what she was experiencing. She'd phoned the law office where she worked as a paralegal to call in sick. It would be impossible to function there under these conditions.

She lit candles. She put out two bowls of water and tried a light meditation, but nothing was helping.

Breathing deeply, she sunk onto the overstuffed moss green love seat that her Aunt Elise had given her when she moved in. She sat cross-legged and attempted to clear her mind in a meditation. But almost in a flood as powerful as the emotions, the images began to pour forth.

She sighed deeply. Of course, the strange quiet girl — one apartment and two to the left over hers. There was a darkness all around her. A self-proclaimed Wiccan, she'd been attempting spells to bind the boyfriend to her—the one that lived there on occasion.

Delia something was her name. They'd introduced themselves once, but she was abominable in remembering last names. "Remember, you have to take extreme precautions when you move out, Caroline," her mother had said. "You're not like other people."

What an extraordinary understatement, but she had to leave, had to leave the safe cocoon of her mother's lovely, sprawling Queen Anne-style house on Prytania Street. Certainly, it would have been easy enough to bury herself there with her mom and her younger brother Jared who seemed more than content to set up shop in the great house for another millennium.

But not her. Caroline Breslin would strike out on her own. Now that she was twenty-five, she would find a way to deal with the pesky problem of being bombarded with other people's emotions.

Again, she attempted to clear her mind, and the dark mucky energy flooding through Delia, what's her name's apartment, seemed to hit its mark on her forehead, exacerbating her headache. "Damn," she exploded, rubbing the sensitive spot. This was not going to work, and it wouldn't due having sick days at her job. Luckily it was Friday, and she had the rest of the weekend to find a solution, short of moving.

She picked up her purse and sunglasses, heading out the front door with no clue where she was going.

◆

The pull led him through the library's wide, dark wood lobby. To either side were massive ornate reading rooms. One was clearly a dining room from long ago with a high, ornately decorated ceiling and a massive marble fireplace. Across the hall, a similarly fashioned parlor was now filled with tables and racks of newspapers.

But he walked past, past the long desk and in the opposite direction of an imposing, black wood staircase that led up to the second floor.

As he continued to the back of the building, the walls became lighter, the décor less formal, and of course, shelves and shelves of books.

He'd remembered being here several times before. Once for a meeting of local small business owners and once for a book sale concentrated on the grounds. If he'd wandered this library area before, it hadn't made an impression. As he drifted into one of the side reading rooms, another doorway compelled him.

Without hesitation, he crossed the threshold, and the light flooded toward him. It was a lovely little nook, a sunroom surrounded by glass walls and filled with wicker chairs, one with a high-rounded back that wouldn't have been out of place on a tropical island. And not unexpectedly, it was occupied.

◆

It helped just getting out of the apartment. Clearly, Delia Whoever was the problem. What she hated was that she'd become "her" problem. Again, the complaint circled to a familiar theme—"It wasn't fair. Why couldn't I be like everyone else?"

Over the years, she'd thought she'd made peace with this reality. Her mother and aunt's approach had always been— "You're gifted for a reason Caroline. Don't treat it like a curse." It was the psychic strain that ran throughout their family. Her brother Jared was a remarkable precognitive. Her Aunt Elise, amongst her many psychic gifts, she'd always found to be a walking lie detector—having an uncanny ability of nearly reading thoughts. And, of course, her mother was a healer, a gift she didn't develop until after their father died nearly a decade before.

But her gift was a different animal. It was almost as if she had to erect artificial barriers where the natural separation of one human begins, and another ends. Usually, she was moderately successful, but not today. It was the energy thing, a new developing facet of her gift of being so cognizant of energy patterns.

She'd decided to go visit her mother's house on Prytania Street this morning. There was always a calming energy there, and maybe her Aunt Elise, a frequent visitor, might just come up with a solution to her particular predicament. This was what she'd decided, but on her way, she took a turn onto St. Charles Avenue on a whim. And on another whim, she impulsively decided to stop at the Milton Latter Library. It was a lovely old building—the house and grounds took up an entire street block. Once the reported mansion of a silent film star in the 1920s, it was one of the few sprawling private residences on St. Charles that was now open to the public.

She hadn't been in the place for years, and as she stepped out of her car, the sky rumbled overhead. Best to get inside soon. Besides, the place was beckoning her, feeling particularly welcoming today. Maybe she could clear her mind, perhaps find a solution on her own. How refreshing that would be not to have to turn to her family for help.

The heavy dark interior flooded toward her as she walked into the front foyer. On either side of her were open doors to lush rooms converted into reading centers but still beautiful and opulent as they must have been in the day. She wandered further within, immediately greeted by an employee at the front desk asking if she needed assistance.

Excellent question, she thought to herself but politely declined rather aimlessly drifting into one of the reading rooms on the left. But then she began to feel it, the pull to another doorway within the room and unexpectedly a burst of light. It was a lovely sunroom decorated with light wicker furniture, and to her extreme delight, it was unoccupied. She settled into an oversized, white wicker chair facing a wall-size window. Allowing herself to relax, she tried to clear her mind and reach out for guidance.

♦

It was perplexing this particular situation. Max had great control of his gifts, at least at times. There were half a dozen murder cases that the New Orleans police force had consulted him on. All were handled privately, quietly behind the scenes, as well as other cases, mostly missing persons. He didn't seek notoriety, and the truth was the police didn't want the news leaking out that they were consulting a psychic. But he was at times called to use his gifts and sometimes strongly.

And then there were the dreams.

The woman with the long reddish-brown hair and green eyes — he couldn't pinpoint the first time he'd seen her, maybe a year before, maybe two. It was random at first, a girl in the background, coming into his bookstore but not speaking, looking intently as though she were searching for something. Then in the last few months, things changed. She'd moved closer.

And, of course, this week, every night, the same dream, like a mantra.

"What do you need?" he asked somberly.

They stood out on the lakefront, and the sky was a startling splash of turquoise. He had a habit of dreaming in vivid, often dramatic colors.

"It's getting worse," she murmured. She'd begun speaking to him just the month before. "I can't keep the walls up. Everything bleeds into my mind now, my skin."

"Your gifts are expanding. It's a transition process. Be patient." He spoke as he felt, although he had no concrete reason for saying so.

"It's driving me crazy. And there's something else."

"Yes, I know. I've felt it coming for some time."

Today the pull had been strong, but he hadn't understood until just this moment what precisely was pulling him. He stood on the threshold of the sunroom staring with a measure of surprise but also understanding at the woman sitting in front of the plate glass window with her eyes closed. She wasn't sleeping. That much he knew. She was in a very light meditation. Then slowly, her eyes opened, lovely wide green eyes, and she stared at him with a touch of recognition.

"Who are you?" she whispered.

He smiled, his awareness embracing the recognition. "I'm Max."

THE DREAM

2

"Who is he?"

Her mother looked at her quizzically. It was perhaps eight months earlier, just before she moved out of the Prytania Street house into her place. She had cornered her mother as she worked diligently on potting some herbal plants out in the greenhouse she'd built after Caroline's father passed away.

Cassie Breslin, whose gloved hands were covered in fine dirt, looked up from her activity with indulgence and confusion.

"I don't know, darling. These are your dreams, after all."

"Yes but—" she faltered in her thoughts, having difficulty making anything coherent from her feelings.

Cassie Breslin had lovely blue eyes, blue like the sky overhead and sometimes blue like the sky before a storm. But now her full attention focused on her daughter's face. "Tell me again about the dream."

Caroline swallowed on a dry throat, hearing that subtle change in pitch in her mother's tone that told her they'd moved into a more serious realm. It was a realm where Cassie would use all her focus and unique talents to unravel this mystery. "Well, I've seen him before. I mean, there was a familiarity. I can't really remember, but I think in dreams."

"Go on," her mother coached. Her eyes were not directly on Caroline now. They seemed to be fixing on some spot beyond her.

"Last night, I dreamed I was walking down a street filled with shops. But I don't think it was around here. It felt sort of like the beach. You know the sea air, and it was cold. And I was wrapped up in some long shawl, rose-colored."

"Emotions," her mother murmured.

"And then I stopped in front of a store, and it was filled with crystals in the window — amethysts, quartz, citrine, great huge chunks of them on display. And they felt powerful."

"Energy," her mother responded from a distant place.

"So, I went inside the door, and the shop was filled with light and books, shelves and shelves of books. I hadn't expected that because it didn't look that way from the outside."

"Knowledge," her mother's voice. "What's next?"

"That's when I saw him. This man walked from behind a counter right up to me, and I knew, well, that I knew him some-how. He said something like *"Don't worry, the time is coming."*

Her mother focused back on her face. "What else?"

She shook her head, "I don't know. I know it went on longer. I know we talked, but I can't remember now."

"So, tell me, Caroline. What did you feel about him?"

She tried to concentrate, and the image came back clearly — brown hair to nearly ash blonde, light eyes, a beard, and mustache. He seemed older than her, but not so much, six or seven years. She wasn't sure. "I don't know. I felt like I should know him and that I will, eventually."

Her mother's lovely blue eyes sharpened a bit. "Is that all?"

Caroline shrugged, "Of course, what else could there be?"

Her mother went back to work on her potting murmuring. "Whatever happened to that fellow Liam that you were seeing?"

"Oh, I don't know. I guess we drifted apart." Cassie nodded, again saying nothing but saying so much while she was saying nothing. "So, what do you think? About the dream?"

"I think it was a definite contact, and sooner or later, you'll see him again."

♦

Her heart clutched in surprise. There he was in the flesh, looking down at her with a smile on his handsome face. "Max," she echoed.

He nodded, "Yes, sorry to disturb you."

She straightened up nervously in the wicker chair and noted distractedly that it had started to rain outside. "No, that's all right." How exactly did one handle such a situation when someone literally walks out of your dreams into the real world?

"Mind if I join you?" he indicated a chair not far from hers that he pulled up next to her. "Well, I suppose this seems odd."

"I've seen you before," she stammered a bit.

"Yes, I know. In fact, I've seen you quite a bit lately, nearly every night."

"Every night? You mean in dreams."

With another smile, she could feel things, so many things from him. It was like being overloaded with impressions. He was staring at her strangely. She could feel, feel his energy closer than his physical body. "What are you doing?" she asked abruptly. An odd expression crossed his face.

"Just trying to feel," he murmured. "Caroline."

"You know my name?"

"Part of it."

"Caroline Breslin," she supplied. She didn't want him rooting around in her mind to get the rest of it. "Are you a psychic or something?"

"Or something, and you, I take it, are a profoundly gifted—"

"Sensitive."

"Empath," he substituted.

"I don't know if I would agree with that."

He smiled again. She was amusing him. He turned from her, deeply focusing on the rain pouring down outside for a moment. "So why are we here, Caroline Breslin? I have the distinct impression that you called me."

"I called you? And how exactly did I do that? I don't really know you at all."

"Don't really? Well, no, I suppose in traditional terms, you don't really. But that doesn't change the fact that I was called, pulled here this morning by you — conscious or not. So, what exactly seems to be the problem?"

"Well," she hesitated, startled by his directness. How perplexing. Would she divulge to this stranger what was going on in her life or not?

And then beyond unexpectedly, quite shockingly to her, he took her hand. "It's all right, Caroline," he murmured. "You might as well make use of me since I'm here."

She frowned, feeling awkwardly confused. "It's complicated. That's why I'm here, trying to figure out what to do."

"It involves—" he coaxed smoothly.

"Someone in my apartment complex," she muttered quickly. "I can't shut them out."

She heard him breathing deeply beside her, concentrating. "You're feeling their emotions."

"Yes, energy, I can usually find a way to separate, but something's wrong."

He was silent. And then, "It must be overwhelming."

"I," softly he squeezed her hand, "yes, it gets to be too much."

"I've never met anyone with your particular abilities before. I can't imagine how you've coped." Slowly, she extracted her hand from his grasp. This was too much, for lack of a better word, intimacy so quickly. He responded, "I didn't mean that as an insult. I am amazed. That's all."

"Well, we do what we have to, I suppose."

He stared at her for a moment as though carefully considering. "If you give me a little time, I might be able to help, Caroline."

"Time? What does that mean?"

"The day, spend the day with me."

"Well," she thought to offer an excuse but was hit again by the weight of her predicament. If he could help, and that was a big if, she needed to try.

◆

The rain had subsided, so they decided to take a walk, or rather he decided. For good or ill, he was taking the lead in this curious business. He hadn't intended to spend the day away from the bookstore, but things were evolving well outside his realm of anticipation.

"Are you all right?"

"Yes, fine." She was nervous. Why wouldn't she be? He was virtually a stranger who was insisting on being privy to very private matters that he was getting the impression that she shared with virtually no one.

Defensive? Yes. Protective of herself? Undeniably. And she was beautiful, striking, mysterious—not just physically. There was a quality to her movement, her speech, and her presence that he found compelling and relaxing, oddly enough. Something he'd found to be extraordinarily rare in his experience. "Where did you say we're going?"

"Coffee shop, not far, just a few blocks down St. Charles."

"Oh, that's right." Distracted, he could feel that dark energy still affecting her. It had seeped in. It was vitally important to find a way to dispel it.

"Do you work?" he asked.

"Um, yes, I'm a paralegal at a firm on Baronne Street. I," hesitating, "well, I called in sick this morning. I felt so bad."

"It's physical?"

"It gets that way — bad headaches, exhaustion, and then all the upset."

"I'm sorry. That must be difficult to deal with," he murmured. He could see more as she spoke, the impressions flooding in more concretely. She didn't respond, just continued to walk. "I have a bookstore on Magazine Street."

She stopped for a moment unexpectedly. "Really? That's strange. I remember you in a bookstore. But it was near the beach, the water."

He smiled, "Now that would be wonderful. I visit the Gulf Coast often." He pointed ahead. "It's not far now."

13

"That sounds like a wonderful business to have." There was something in her voice, envy, sadness, evidently not so content at the law firm.

"Yes, it suits me well."

The Bookstore

3

They sat out on the patio for privacy after the waitress had dried off the wrought iron table and chairs from the rain. Caroline's headache had passed, and she was feeling calmer. And distantly, she wondered if this was her companion's doing. He was in many ways an extraordinary man—seemingly very low key, relaxed, but extraordinarily perceptive. She could feel it just being near him, great depths that he kept guarded and was keeping guarded from her as well.

She sipped from her hot cup of café au lait, which was helpful as the morning rain had brought a light chill into the air. "It seems like there are two problems here, Caroline." She slowly placed the mug on the table, focused entirely on Maximilian Gravier, or Max as he said he preferred to be called. She still had no idea why he was here—why she felt she should trust him. All of it was strangely unnerving and had a profoundly unreal quality to it.

"Do you do this often? Help people you don't know?"

He looked a bit bemused at the question. "Yes, I have helped people before. I've helped the police solve cases and others. But have I ever helped someone under these particular circumstances? I'd have to say no."

"Why? I mean why do you do it? Do you feel it's a calling or something?"

He sipped his coffee. She was searching, wanting something. "Haven't you ever used your gifts to help people, Caroline?"

She considered the question. "I don't know. When I was young, my aunt and I would go out, and she would ask me to feel about certain people. I think maybe she tried to help them. I'm not sure. For me, it's just been a battle of trying to manage, you know, trying to live. It would be nice to turn it to some positive purpose. I'm sorry that I stopped you. You were saying two problems."

"Are you feeling better?"

She nodded, "Yes, I feel much calmer, thank you."

"Good, yes, well, as I was saying, there seem to be two problems. The first is the most pressing."

"You mean the girl upstairs."

"Yes, we need to block the effects of her activity from you."

"And the other?"

"Well, the other is you. You need to find a way not to be so, for lack of a better word, vulnerable."

"So," she sighed deeply, completely overwhelmed, "how do we do any of this?"

"Well, let's finish our coffee, then stop by my store. I may have some things there that might help."

She smiled at him, feeling a curious kinship with this man. "I want you to know how much I appreciate your efforts."

"Max."

"Yes, Max, I'm glad we met."

◆

She'd followed him in her car to Magazine Street. She'd checked her watch, only 10:30 AM, although it felt as though so much time had passed. On the drive, her cell phone rang. Quickly, she answered it, seeing that it was her mom, instinctively knowing that if she didn't, there would be follow-up calls.

"Caroline, are you all right? I just had a strange feeling about you today."

Her mother was too perceptive, particularly where she was concerned. "Yes, I'm fine. Look, a lot's going on today, but I promise I will call you later and fill you in. I hate talking on this thing when I'm driving."

"You're driving? Aren't you at work?"

Great, opening a can of worms, "No, I called in sick."

"You're sick? Then why are you—"

"Mom, it's complicated. I promise, later."

Silence on the other end, clearly, this didn't sit too well with her. "All right, be careful." And then she hung up. Sometimes it was so easy to piss her mom off. She did it often, having no idea why. He drove a jeep, a black one. She parallel parked behind him on a side street just off of Magazine.

"Everything all right?" he asked as she joined him on the sidewalk.

Good lord, she was beginning to see that there were way too many psychics in the building.

◆

There was light, light everywhere. This was the first thing that hit her as she walked into Gravier's Bookshop. Of course, it looked nothing like the dream except for the fact that she could breathe more freely.

"How long have you been here?"

"Here?" he responded. He was behind a long dark wood counter on the side of the ground floor. There were at least two floors that she knew of. Of course, she hadn't been upstairs yet. "Um, we bought the building about six years ago."

"We?" she asked, a little surprised. Ever since she had come into contact with Max, she'd sensed he was alone, not attached.

"Yes, my wife and I."

It came as a jolt. She wasn't usually so far afield. "I didn't know you were married."

He glanced up from a stack of mail he'd picked up on the way into the shop. "I was married. My wife passed away three years ago."

She stared at him, transfixed for a moment, then felt a swift rush around her from the walls, the books, and from him. There was that veil that seemed to hold him just slightly aloof, and now she could see it was grief. "I'm sorry. I didn't realize."

"Well, this isn't about me," he said calmly. "Let's see if we can find anything in here that might be helpful to you. I keep a collection upstairs."

She eyed him with curiosity. "Collection of what, dragons?"

A slight smile flickered across his slightly tanned face. "Well, that could be one interpretation."

◆

They'd had a dream, he and his college sweetheart Chloe. They lived in a small shotgun house on Calhoun Street but invested money in buying the building that would house the bookstore on Magazine Street. He'd found that sometimes a common goal could be the glue that held two people together. Not that they wouldn't have held together otherwise because he loved his wife dearly, although he knew on some level that it wasn't a perfect mesh.

He'd studied history at Tulane University and had even penned several books on the city's past. Chloe had majored in visual arts, toying with opening her own gallery after establishing the bookstore. But as events unfolded, there had been only time for one dream.

Unexpectedly stricken with a heart condition, she weakened and finally slipped away from him at age thirty-two. He left the house on Calhoun and moved into the second floor on Magazine Street. In the solitude of his grief, he started paying attention to what his late wife would call "unnatural inclinations." He launched into a study of the occult, which deepened his understanding of his capabilities.

The girl, as he had begun to call her in his mind, although he estimated she was just a decade his junior, followed him up the wooden staircase to the second floor of the building. He'd placed French doors at the top of the landing, which he unlocked, leading her into his domain.

The upstairs consisted of three rooms: a small den with an open kitchen, a study, and a bedroom. Photographs that Chloe had taken around the city still hung on the walls. Caroline hesitated in front of them as though absorbing. "In here," he directed rather abruptly.

Her green eyes flew to his face with a bit of surprise. He didn't want her digging too deeply into his life, trying to glean an understanding of things that he still didn't completely understand.

Silently, she followed behind him. The study was a large spacious room with doors that led out onto a small balcony patio. "This is quite a place," she murmured.

Against the wall were shelves that he'd put in, some protected with glass and others open. Her eyes widened as she began to take in what was there, a collection of items — crystals, amulets, knives, swords, statues, and very old books. She moved closer, "There's a lot of power here," she commented, her voice a bit distant.

Caroline Breslin drifted toward the shelves, almost trance-like, seemingly mesmerized. Fortunately, he was standing so near her, able to catch her fall when she collapsed.

CHLOE

4

I t was overwhelming, the shift in energies that enveloped her. She had felt it the moment that she crossed the threshold of *Gravier's Bookshop* on Magazine Street. It was dizzying, disorienting, but it wasn't until they ascended the stairs that she could pinpoint the source. Max's private collection virtually hummed with energy.

"Where did you get these things?" she asked, or had she? Perhaps she was asking now. She'd fallen into a blanket of darkness and then into an impossibly huge room with ceilings that seemed to reach the sky.

"Where are you going?"

"I've no idea," she whispered. There were glittering crystal chandeliers reflecting, refracting light into rainbows across the black and white mosaic floor. Everything gleamed.

"These are things that need to be understood," a voice she didn't recognize.

"By me?" she asked no one in particular because no one was there, no one in the flesh.

"By many, by you both, it's why you were brought together."

She felt another rush of dizziness as she looked to the ceiling. It was blinding. And then she opened her eyes, and the room's light stung painfully.

She squeezed them shut in reflex and then slowly flickered them open again. She felt the pressure of him holding her hand, touching her face with his other hand. "Caroline, are you all right?" His voice was strong, soothing, wrapping around her in comfort.

She focused slowly on his face. "I passed out?" she murmured, more of a question than a statement.

He looked at her a little oddly. "You did," he remarked quietly. "How are you feeling?"

She hesitated, "Oh foolish, but okay, I think." She tried to sit up, but his hands moved to her shoulders softly, pressuring her to lie back down. "Better give yourself a minute. How about I get you something to drink?"

She closed her eyes for a second and, in her mind, saw the great room again with the rainbows on the floor. The dizziness still clung to her. "Maybe so," she answered.

He stood up from a small wooden stool he'd evidently pulled up next to her, saying firmly while putting it aside. "Don't get up until I get back," and then he'd left. Well, she found that a bit pushy given their very limited acquaintance. Shakily, dismissing his advice, she managed to sit up. Across the room were the shelves with all those mystical items that had flung her into this perplexing state.

She recognized now that she'd been lounging on a sort of couch that she hadn't even noticed when she first entered the room. Checking her watch, she noted it was after eleven. What a perfectly bizarre day this was eroding into, starting with her forced flight from her apartment this morning. And to culminate, she ended up in a faint on the sofa of a virtual stranger having visions of some palatial, glittering room.

She was not the fainting kind. In fact, she couldn't remember ever fainting before. She sighed deeply, before this.

Caroline shifted, swinging her feet down to the wooden floor, still dizzy, still seeing rainbows flickering from that other place. In some ways, she felt like she was in that grand room, feeling the chill, with its strange energies emanating from so many places. It was powerful and still had a hold on her.

Then she heard the stairs creaking, and Max walked through the French doors with a bottle in his hand. "You don't listen," he commented with a touch of humor.

"No, not generally."

"Well, here, drink this," he said, handing her a very icy bottle of what turned out to be root beer.

"Thanks," she said, taking a frothy sip whose sugar seemed to shoot right into her veins. The jolt did seem to aid in pulling her back to the present.

"Helping?" he asked, sitting next to her on the sofa.

"Definitely, sorry about that. I don't usually faint at anything."

"So, you said," he answered quietly.

"It felt," then she stopped. Was it wise to be so candid with this man? It had always been her practice to be discreet about her psychic impressions, except around her family.

"It felt—" he echoed. "You know, Caroline, sooner or later, you'll have to decide to trust me."

"Because?" she murmured, sipping the powerful soda. Traditionally she was a diet drinker, so this was an unusual treat.

"Because that's the only way I can help you."

"You really think you can help me, Max?" she asked, meeting his eyes directly.

He hesitated as though he were considering carefully. "I don't know, but I am sure going to try."

She nodded slowly, then turned away. It was a bit unsettling to engage his gaze. It felt like it linked them in a way she had no clue what to do with. "Your collection, the energies I felt, hit me hard."

"Made you faint?"

"Propelled me into some sort of vision."

"What vision?" he asked directly.

◆

He went for a walk down the street to a local restaurant to pick up two shrimp po'boys for lunch. He'd insisted Caroline continue to rest until he returned. Of course, as things were going, he had no idea whether or not she would heed his advice. His short exposure to her had shown that she followed her inclinations to the exclusion of most other things.

He tried hard to clear his thoughts. Things were getting complicated and layered. Her issues at her apartment seemed entirely separate from the vision of the ballroom, for lack of a better description, that she'd seen during her faint. It seemed so, but then a wise mentor had told him once: *"Everything is connected and touches everything else. Like a stone tossed into a pond, the ripples expand far beyond what the eyes can perceive."*

So, what were the ripples, and what was the stone here? The Magazine Street Po'boy Shop was at least four blocks down from his bookstore, and how he needed those four blocks. There were so many colliding impressions, as though he'd opened Pandora's Box, and all manner of things were flooding out now.

He forced his mind to clear, wondering vaguely what Chloe would have made of all of this.

His thoughts drifted back into a familiar groove—the lovely face of his deceased wife.

"What do you think of this?" he'd asked, holding up a painting he'd acquired just a day earlier from an art show in the French Quarter.

She was sitting in a chair near a window in the bookshop. Lately, she seemed to crave being near the light. It disturbed him how frail she'd become and how distant. She was on a waiting list for a heart transplant. The doctors reassured them any day now, but lately, any day seemed to stretch further and further away.

Her soft brown eyes seemed glazed. She'd been somewhere else. He tried hard to suppress that truth, but at times, it was undeniable. "What did you say?" she murmured.

He laughed, not to let her know how deeply troubled he was. "I see. I just can't get your attention these days, my love."

She smiled with that gently sad smile of hers. "I'm sorry," then her eyes focused on the painting of Pirate's Alley. "I like it. Very authentic."

"But where to hang it?"

"Maybe upstairs in the unfinished rooms. I can see you living there," and then she hesitated, confused, "sometimes."

He squatted in front of her chair, taking her cool hand in his. "Now, why would I do that?" he asked in the light, jovial tone he'd adopted lately. "We have a lovely house on Calhoun Street."

"I know, but sometimes I see it, you in those rooms." She closed her eyes for a moment.

He squeezed her hand, "Can I get you anything?"

They flickered open again. "I love you, Max."

"I know," he said, kissing her hand.

She nodded, "I'm not sad, just tired. This body feels so tired."

"It's all right," he murmured. He wanted to say don't worry. Any day there would be a transplant. But the words felt hollow, and she would hear them. These days she heard Everything.

"I'm sorry, Max."

He looked at her with confusion. "Sorry for what, Chloe?"

She shook her head. "I didn't understand before. You have to see. You have to use your gifts."

A lump formed in his throat. He'd made that choice once he married Chloe—all his psychic inclinations would remain buried. He held her hand more tightly. "That's not important now."

"No, it is," her voice sounded distant, transformed in some way. "It's what you need to do. I can see it now. There will be people to help you. Let them in. There will be," and then she paused as though gathering her thoughts. "There will be people to love you, Max, just like I did. Let them in."

And then he remembered she had begun to speak of other things, mundane things, as though the entire conversation had not taken place.

◆

"What's going on? I'm worried about you."

Caroline leaned back on Maximilian Gravier's sofa and contemplated how to explain what was happening to her psychic mother. "I'm all right. I just took a sick day off from work. I needed to sort some things out."

Silence at the other end of her cell phone, "Where are you, baby?"

This was tricky, no deliberate lies, but too much truth would open the whole can of worms. "I'm in a bookstore on Magazine Street. Ever been here?"

"So, you're not sick?"

"Not physically. Like I said, I have some things to sort out. Once I do, I'll be ready to talk about it."

"That's very cryptic, darling." She sighed. Her mother wasn't buying it, but she didn't have time for this right now—too much to deal with. "Is it nice?"

"What?"

"The bookstore, what did you call it?"

"Oh yeah, Gravier's Bookshop."

"Do they have much of a metaphysical section?"

"Um, I'm not sure. I'll poke around and let you know."

"Well, I guess I'll let you go. Sure you don't need anything?"

She glanced around, distantly hearing a front door downstairs opening and closing. "No, I'm good. I'll call you tonight."

"Fine," she hung up. Lovely, she really needed complications. And then Max suddenly appeared on the threshold, crossing through the French doors with a bag in his hand.

"Everything all right?" he asked, clearly eying the cell phone.

She smiled, "Yeah, um, do you have a metaphysical section?"

CRYSTALS

5

They ate largely in silence on the balcony that led out from the upstairs bedroom in the bookstore. Max had placed a small wrought iron table with two chairs for such occasions. But as he'd found since he'd moved in, occasions for actually using it were few and far between.

After Chloe passed away, he'd become fairly reclusive, although a well-meaning friend had insisted on setting him up once, in fact, not so very long ago. She was actually a lovely lady, a tall, striking brunette who was an instructor of music at Loyola University. She was an excellent conversationalist, well-read, upbeat, everything one could want in a woman except that he didn't want it. They'd spoken a few more times on the phone after the dinner, then not again. While having all these other fine qualities, she was perceptive as well. It was painfully clear to him now that it would take something extraordinary to urge him to connect emotionally with a woman again.

Now eying his present companion across the patio table, he recognized that Caroline Breslin seemed lost in her own oppressive world at the moment. She stared off distantly and toyed with a French fry that she had twice brought up to her mouth, then absently had returned it to its former residence among a pile of fellow French fries on a napkin.

"Enjoying your lunch?" he murmured in a friendly tone.

Her eyes returned to him from that distant place of worry. "Yeah, it's great."

"You haven't eaten much." He noted congenially. She was moody, and he'd decided the best way to handle her right now was to stay calm and be affable.

She glanced down at the food before her as though suddenly acknowledging its existence. A third of the sandwich was gone, and at tops half a dozen French fries. "Oh, it's good, but I'm just not that hungry. It's been a strange day."

"You should eat some more. We have a lot of work to do this afternoon. You're going to need to have a clear mind."

"And food will accomplish this?" Again, worry seemed to flicker across her lovely forehead. She was pretty. Even he, the reclusive widower he was, had to admit that, pretty and kind of funny in her way. "What kind of work?" she asked, following up on her sarcastic food comment.

He took a substantial bite out of a French fry before answering. Nothing wrong with his appetite. "We need to head over to your apartment and see if we can make some sense of things."

She frowned, "You really think this is a good idea?"

"It's a place to start." She nodded dubiously, staring blankly at her food. She was depressed. He could feel it. Instinctively, he put his hand on her arm, and she looked up with large lovely green eyes. "It'll be all right. You're not alone."

She held his gaze momentarily, then returned to eating her lunch. This time with just a tad more enthusiasm.

◆

It was nearly one o'clock when Caroline opened the door of her Carrollton Avenue apartment. Before they'd left his bookshop, Max had insisted that she take a few moments to clear her mind and surround herself with white light in a sort of meditation nook that he'd set up in one of the many back rooms of Gravier's Bookshop. There was a rug on the floor that reminded her a bit of the Southwest and a small antique-looking trunk with a candle atop as well as various crystals. He'd insisted that they sit on the floor and meditate.

"Do you meditate every day?" he'd inquired.

"No, not every day."

"You know, for someone like you, it's important to keep balance."

"Life gets busy."

"That's why it's essential."

She'd watched as he'd sat down on the rug, cross-legged, then eyed her expectantly. "Come on," he'd said calmly.

"You know, I'm not one of those yoga people."

"This isn't yoga," he'd said. But she'd done it, awkward as she felt, beside him. Now she'd spent a lot of time around men, her brother, lawyers at work, and a random boyfriend here and there, but Max Gravier, she had to say, was sexy. Not in an obvious way. There was a self-assurance about him, a quiet command, and a sensuality that he just kind of emanated without trying. She'd met guys and hesitated to use the word men in conjunction with those who tried to be smooth and appear confident but just came off as false or overbearing. But Max, he simply was, and what she also felt that he simply was still very involved with his deceased wife. So, she deliberately quelled such musings. He was unattainable in the worst way possible. His object of affection wasn't around to compete with.

"What do we do?" she whispered, settling next to him on the rug.

"What do you normally do when you meditate?"

"I try to clear my mind of all thought."

"Sounds good," he answered. How could one feel nervous and relaxed next to someone simultaneously? Focus, focus, Caroline, she commanded herself.

She breathed deeply, trying to let the day's anxiety slip away. It was anxiety that looked like her mother, her job, her apartment, that great big glittery room, all of it. She just pushed to let it all go.

"You need to protect yourself."

"Hmm?" she answered, eyes still closed, in puzzlement.

"Surround yourself with white light and ask for protection."

"Okay," she concentrated on the image of white light all around her, surrounding her. But it began to creep in, a feeling of sadness, loneliness here—the feelings of struggling to keep hold of emotions.

"Stop it."

"What?" she said.

"Focus, Caroline, don't allow other people's emotions to creep up on you."

"What? I?"

"You have to learn to build more control."

She sighed deeply, "Okay, I'm trying." Mentally she brushed it away, and focused on the light around her, the white light that was building a wall.

"Better," he said beside her.

Yes, it was better.

◆

Max was cautious. He'd brought some pieces of crystal from his collection but nothing else. Something in it triggered a bad reaction within Caroline, and he didn't have time to analyze it. After the meditation, he'd collected what was necessary and followed her in his car to her apartment. He'd closed the bookshop for an entire day, but he felt it was warranted. At least, he hoped it was warranted. He planned to settle her immediate problems and send her on her way. He didn't plan any extended association here. What was clear was that she was a gifted empath, perhaps more. And from what she'd indicated, she had others in her family who could also lend support. So, there wouldn't be a need for him, and he could resume his own life at his leisure.

These were the things he told himself. Now whether he believed them or not was entirely a different matter.

He'd parked his Jeep on the street several spots down from Caroline's car. As was the case in much of the city, street parking was all that was available here. She was waiting for him on the sidewalk. Her eyes focused intently on the greenish-gray cement building before her. So intent was her concentration that she didn't even acknowledge him when he walked up beside her.

"Be careful," he told her.

Finally, her eyes met his, misty, overcome with impressions. "What?"

"You have to protect yourself, Caroline. Remember the white light. Don't just let impressions have free rein over your mind."

She spoke softly, "I'm not looking forward to this."

"It's all right. I'll help." He stated rather stoically. He was steeling himself. Unfortunately, he could feel tangibly there was more here than met the eye.

She looked at him for a moment dubiously, then began to head for the front door of the complex. Max followed closely, still carrying the small tote bag filled with crystals.

THE APARTMENT

6

As Caroline unlocked the front door of her ground-level apartment, she tried to focus on what had drawn her to this place initially—the light, the thick cement walls that somehow felt like protection, and the lovely patio.

Mentally she tried to do as Max suggested. She clothed herself in white light in positive thoughts as her Aunt Elise had always insisted.

As she reached to turn the doorknob, she felt Max's hand close over hers gently, stilling her progress. "Hold on," he murmured. She looked up into his face. But his eyes were closed in concentration.

"What?" she whispered a bit harshly in distraction. And then his eyes opened, still staring forward with intense focus and determination.

"This is more complicated than I thought."

"What does that mean?"

He spoke quietly, "There's something in there."

Her eyes widened. "Should I call the police?"

He shook his head, "No, they couldn't see it. But it appears your friend from upstairs has released something—something that now exists between."

Panic flew up into her heart. "What! What the hell is it doing in my apartment?"

"Seeking energy, I'd imagine. Seeking the strongest energy it can in order to exist."

"I don't understand," she whispered in a high-pitched panic. "Is she that smart that she could create something?"

"Probably not," although he did not sound entirely convincing, "probably an accident. Go ahead inside."

Her eyes widened more, "Are you kidding?"

"We must get rid of it."

"What? How are we supposed to—"

Looking at her intently, he said flatly. "You want me to go first?"

"Yes," she answered emphatically, "yes, that would be nice."

He gently pushed her out of the way and gave her a final glance before he moved forward. "Settle down, Caroline. It'll be fine."

"Right, easy for you to say. You don't have a thing in your apartment." She muttered.

♦

About a year after Chloe left him, Max began to become aware of the invisible beings that shared space with us on planet Earth. Chartres Street first introduced him to the concept of interdimensional beings.

"Some of them are as inconsequential as insects. The way that mosquitoes feed on blood, these feed on energy, life auras for their sustenance."

"Where do they come from?"

"Unfortunately, often from us, what we fail to realize is how powerful we are. No thought form is so weak that it doesn't have some end result. Thought is energy, the power of creation. And unmonitored thoughts create chaos."

"You lost me."

She'd smiled, a local visiting medium from out west named Hilda Wilder. "It's a difficult concept. But let's just say that over the course of history—very positive events have created positive energy—and sometimes beings of that order."

"And negative?"

"Yes, well, it's true there has been too much unchecked negative energy and its unfortunate results."

◆

He steeled himself as he walked into the den of Caroline Breslin's apartment. He had spent extensive time fine-tuning his sensibilities so that these sorts of creations could be on his radar. Some particularly destructive ones were categorized as poltergeists. But this one, he frowned. This one was focused and set loose on her for a particular purpose.

The room that had been in shadows moments before was now flooded in light. He heard Caroline behind him softly close the door, but he didn't look at her or take in any particular details about him. He simply focused, focused in on tuning himself into a very particular level of energy vibration.

"Anything?" she whispered behind him.

"Quiet," he murmured in a soft voice. He could follow the threads now, low dark threads of energy that were nearly imperceptible, nearly. It was quiet now, definitely trying to hide.

He let the bag of crystals softly drop onto the carpeted floor of her den and walked across the room to a closed doorway.

"That's my—" then she stopped speaking.

Quite deliberately, he reached for the doorknob and slowly turned it, opening the darkened room. It was dusky in here as well, but light was not necessary. Of course, there it was, huddled on the bed, buried beneath the covers. Caroline spent so much time there sleeping, so it was drawing from remnants of energy. It looked up at him with wide eyes, not really a sentient being, more akin to an animal simply focused on its need for food. But the face did indeed bear the imprint of its maker.

He felt Caroline's movement behind him. He grabbed her abruptly, swinging her close to the side of him so that she had a clear view of what he was looking at.

"I want you to see this," he whispered.

"It's dark. I can't," she rasped, squirming a bit in the unexpected embrace.

"Open your mind and focus. Feel the energy. Right on the bed," his voice was low and controlling. But this was important, essential. She had to be able to protect herself. She was too vulnerable. He'd sensed that from the moment she'd first entered his dreams. "Focus," he commanded.

"I'm trying," and then he could feel it. With his hands touching her, he could feel the energy shifting, mutating inside her. "I can see something. It looks like a red glow on my bed," she murmured frantically.

"Good, now let it take shape."

He could hear, no, actually feel her breathing steady. "I'm trying. I—" then she stopped.

Then there was terror that seemed to rip right through her. That was, of course, the danger when one first began to see.

"Oh God, what the hell is that?"

"I can only conclude that is your neighbor's creation."

"It's horrible but, but it has her face."

"Clearly, she's tied to it. Any energy it draws from you, she shares in."

"That bitch!" she hissed.

He laughed softly, "Well, now let's get to work."

"Get to work?" she echoed, her voice still laced with disgust.

"Getting rid of it."

♦

He sat next to her on the short sofa given to her by Aunt Elise, holding her hand. But the only image that Caroline Breslin could see in her mind was the creature with the red glow and Delia, whoever she was's face.

"Are you all right?"

"Not really."

"Look, it's not as bad as you think."

"There's a monster on my bed. Even if I get rid of it, how exactly am I supposed ever to sleep there again?"

He sighed or grumbled. She wasn't entirely sure which. "I guess it's a shock, but once you get used to seeing these sorts of things—"

"Are you used to it?"

There was silence. Evidently, she'd made her point. "Do you want to get rid of it?"

"Yes, please," she murmured, and he squeezed her hand reassuringly. She liked holding his hand. It was warm, comforting, tingling, and then she quelled that thought. This was business for him, nothing more.

"We're going to have to approach it on its level."

"You mean hell?"

"No, now close your eyes and focus. We're going to attempt a specific sort of meditation. We're going to enter its plane of existence."

She wasn't sure she understood what he meant and wasn't sure she wanted to. But she did as he asked.

"Now focus, Caroline. Focus on its energy vibration."

She did so, feeling herself slip into a deeper concentration, an altered place where she simply listened. Its energy was like a peculiar low hum, not soothing but raspy, abrasive.

"Can you see it?" He asked somewhere beside her, or perhaps not, perhaps somewhere within.

"No," she answered. "I hear it, but I can't see it yet."

"Try." Geeze, what a taskmaster!

She opened her eyes, or so she thought, but it was all different. The room was buzzing, vibrating, filled with sound frequencies and colors.

"Find it," he coaxed. Her eyes traveled across the den that, for the moment, bore little resemblance to where she spent so much of her time. Finally, after sorting through layers of bending and turning color, she saw the path of red like a translucent rope leading to the bedroom door. "Got it," she told him somehow, but now it all felt like mind communication.

"Good, now you're on its plane. You need to track it." Max was speaking directly to her mind. She could feel him, so close.

She felt herself come to her feet and head toward the bedroom door. But then she stopped and looked back to the sofa. She and Max were still sitting there, eyes closed. "It's all right," she heard him whisper.

She turned. There he was, standing directly beside her, she thought, though his image seemed to flicker in and out. "What's happening?" she asked, although she already suspected having some minimal experience with this.

"Astral selves, bodies still where we left them. Go on, open the door."

She reached down to turn the knob, but it didn't quite work. Somehow, she passed right through it. She and, beside her, Max were standing in the bedroom as was the thing—standing up on her bed facing them as though it were ready for battle.

DELIA

1

"**S**teady," she heard him whisper in her mind.

It was hot where they were. She could feel it, heat and irritation. Dizziness swirled through her. "Careful, we're on its plane, but don't get pulled too far in."

It blinked, looking at them from one to another, blinked with Delia's huge eyes. Then she felt the pull, like a distinctive yank. She wasn't in her bedroom anymore.

"Max," she rasped frantically in her mind. But all she heard was a low flutter of disconnected noise. She looked around. It was an apartment not unlike hers except for dramatically different furnishings. She breathed deeply or as much as she could manage. She was in the darkened den, only illuminated by the flickering of a candle—a candle with someone sitting on the floor hunched over it. As she cautiously moved closer, she noted there was a circle around the figure, not drawn but made of—"

"Ash."

She turned to find Max standing beside her. "Sorry took me a minute to catch up."

"What is this?"

"I'd imagine it's the source."

The figure's head came up, and she flung back a mass of long, jet-black hair. Immediately, Caroline recognized the pale face. "Delia."

Delia shakily stood up within the confines of the circle and outstretched her hands, murmuring something from a language Caroline didn't understand. Her arms were trembling and dripping with blood.

"What did she do to herself?" she asked aloud. And then Delia turned as though in response to the question. "She can hear me?"

"She seems to have put herself in an altered state," Max responded. Delia's eyes were wide, looking at them, blinking in a way that disturbingly reminded Caroline of the creature. "Talk to her," Max encouraged.

"And say what exactly?"

"She seems drawn to you. Maybe you can help settle this."

"Wonderful."

"Try. You have many gifts."

She did try. She focused on the pathetic girl standing before her, dripping in blood. "What are you doing, Delia?" She directed to her.

The girl looked at her with confusion, as though she wasn't sure who or what was addressing her. "Are you a spirit?" she asked with fear laced in her voice.

"Say yes."

"Yes, I am. I'm here to help you."

The dark eyes widened. "Will you bring back Tony?"

"Oh my God, is this really all about some guy?" she directed to Max.

"Stay with it. It's her reality, not yours."

"I'm here to help you. You're lost, Delia."

She heard a rasp behind them. "Don't pay attention," Max warned.

"But—"

"Yes, it's here. It's feeling its existence threatened. I'll keep my eye on it. You keep going."

"But things were all right while he was here. I need him back."

Good grief, co-dependent much. "You'll be all right, Delia, but you must stop this."

The eyes hardened a bit. "Stop what?"

"The spells, the cutting, the things that hurt you, all of this will come back to harm you and others. That's not what you want, is it?"

She shook her head, "No, I just need more power. A little more power, and I could pull it together."

Now she could see. That was where she came in, the more power thing. She heard a vicious rasp behind her, then almost a heat on her back, but suddenly a sort of howl. "What did you do?"

"Don't worry about it," Max answered.

"Look, don't tell me—"

"I'm protecting you. Stay focused."

She turned back to Delia, who seemed to have a confused expression on her face. "How many of you are there?" she asked.

"Many," she responded. "Many are watching you and are concerned that you are heading into darkness. This man was not positive for you. Let him go and live your life. You need to do many important things, but you can't if you go down this path."

"That's good, Caroline." She felt Max close to her, his words in her mind. It made her feel stronger somehow.

"But I need this. I need the spells. It makes me different."

Super, low self-esteem—the modern plague of American young women, "No, it's deceptive. You are special, but this takes away from you."

"Show her."

"What?"

"Show her what she has created."

"I want to show you something, Delia. Look closely."

She and Max moved to the side, out of the path of the thing that she felt sure was only steps behind her. She could see Delia's eyes searching the room and then suddenly fixing on it as though her vision had cleared. "Oh God, what is it?"

"This is what your actions have created."

The entity moved forward, and Caroline could feel rage and confusion, but mostly hunger, terrible hunger emanating from it.

"Why does it have my face?"

"Because it is connected to you, it is your creation. You need to set it free."

"What? I don't know how."

Her mind went blank in sheer panic. She was too close. She could feel Delia's complete terror paralyze her. "Max," she reached out.

"It's all right, Caroline. Pull back a bit." Fear and panic were flooding through her. Was this what this girl was feeling? Or was it this thing? It was terrible. "Come on. I'll help you." She could feel the strength and comfort in his voice, and she clung to it. Finally, again the words began to come.

"Tell it you set it free, Delia. That it is no longer bound to you."

She could still feel the icy fear but then heard the words shakily come from the girl. "I'm sorry. I didn't mean to bring pain. I set you free."

"Wish it peace."

"I wish you peace."

Delia stretched out her hand, and the red glowing entity moved toward her hesitantly, then with its appendage brushing her fingers. Caroline almost thought that she heard a perceptible sizzle, then smoke. The thing dissipated and then disappeared.

"What happened?"

"It's gone. It melted back into energy. It was too young to sustain any real form." A mad rush of dizziness flowed through her. "I feel so weak."

"Let's go back."

And in a great flurry of disorientation and then blackness, they returned.

THE BEACH

8

Again, sitting on her sofa in the flesh, and then there was the uncontrollable, wrenching nausea. "I'm sorry," she said as she ran toward the bathroom. All she needed was to be sick in front of the handsome psychic. And she was ill, throwing up until her skin was damp with sweat, and she was shaking all over. What a lovely day off she was having. Giving herself a few moments to rinse her face with water and ensure the surging nausea had passed, she checked her appearance in the mirror. Face pale, eyes with dark circles, all the morning's make-up dissipated somewhere into the cosmos, and long brown hair unruly. But that she brushed out to a controllable status. Oh well, it wasn't like she was trying to snag a date. With a deep breath, she opened the bathroom door and headed out with a quick look at the bed—still unmade, but fortunately, no red glowing creature with her neighbor's face on it.

She left the bedroom to find Max standing near the dinette across the den. He looked at her immediately with a measure of concern. "Are you all right?"

"Um, yeah, just a little sick."

He still looked worried. "I put some coffee on, but I could make tea if you'd rather."

She shook her head, suddenly feeling an unexpected awkwardness now, as though they'd been through something amazingly intimate—and now, well now, it was strange as hell. "Coffee sounds great. I would have made some if, well, if you hadn't already." Her voice kind of drifted off.

"Yeah," he looked odd. Kind of that look her brother got when he had something to say but wasn't at all sure if it would be received well.

"What?" she said directly, unable to tolerate any more uncomfortable silence. And after all, it always seemed to work with Jared.

"So, I think this place is better now. But I put out some crystals to help the energy. You might want to burn some white candles. That thing, well it pulled a bit of energy from here."

"Okay, I don't know how I will sleep here. I still feel creepy," she rambled.

"Oh, don't worry. It's gone, and it will be better."

"Okay, good." What was it? What was he trying to say? If she tried to read him, so to speak, he would feel it. "What about Delia? I mean, will she remember all of this?"

"Possibly, but it might feel more like a dream or fantasy. She won't be certain if it's real, but I'm sure the effect will be profound. I think you scared her into taking another path."

She laughed, "Scared psychically straight, sounds good."

He nodded, still looking at her with concern. "I think you need some rest, Caroline."

That felt abrupt. "I am tired. I'm sure the coffee is almost ready."

He glanced to the kitchen for a moment, then back to her. "I'm going to get going. You might want to spend some time with your family this weekend. It might help with energy."

She nodded, feeling an odd lump of disappointment in her stomach. "Okay," she said, following him to the door. He really seemed anxious to leave. "I don't know how I can thank you, Max. You've done so much for me."

He paused at the door, looking at her a bit strangely. She was finding it difficult to read him just now. Then his hand came up and gently brushed her cheek. "You know where I am if you need anything."

"Yes, *Gravier's Bookshop*," she smiled.

And then he hesitated again before going out the door. "On your bed, you might want to wash those sheets."

She smiled again. "Yeah, my thoughts exactly."

◆

Max left Caroline Breslin's apartment. It was approaching three in the afternoon, although it felt so much later. There was much to process, and he desperately needed to recharge. He needed the beach, thinking seriously about packing a bag and heading out to the Gulf Coast for the weekend. But then he dropped the idea because it made him think about Caroline Breslin and what she needed. How depleted of energy she was, how it would do her great good to get away. Then he stopped.

It would take something extraordinary for him to want to get emotionally close to a woman again. These were his words—how your words come back to bite you. This afternoon he had gotten emotionally close to Caroline Breslin. He'd been in her mind, felt her emotions unvarnished, unprotected, as close as he could. Perhaps even more so than if they'd made love right there on the spot.

Was he stupid for allowing this to happen? He sighed deeply. But how could he know? It had never happened before. He'd lived with Chloe for seven years and never gotten this close to her.

He headed home, back to Magazine Street. He'd spend the rest of the afternoon resting and not thinking about this. He'd have a cold beer, although it was early, and he wouldn't think about this, about all the emotions surging up in him. Emotions he'd no longer believed he was capable of.

◆

There hadn't been time to wash the sheets, just strip the bed, throw them on the floor, and bury herself beneath her thick, light blue, satin comforter. The fatigue had rushed over her quickly, in fact, not long after Max had left. She couldn't soak up what had happened or consider how to proceed now that it had. All she could do now was sleep, sleep a heavy, demanding sleep.

For the first few hours, the blanket of exhaustion fell over Caroline, blocking out everything, particularly any possibility of dreams. But then it shifted, and she found herself walking along the beach in a long white nightgown. Her feet were bare, and the water rushed up about her ankles, just splashing the gown's hem. But she didn't care. In fact, it seemed she didn't care about anything. It all felt wonderful around her.

"It's peaceful here."

"I know," she murmured, answering, not entirely sure who she was answering. But looking down, she noted beside her a pair of masculine feet also aimlessly sloshing in the surf. "Your pants are getting wet." She added with some amusement.

"So, I see," he said in a low voice.

"I thought you were anxious to go home."

She looked up into Max's face—pretty much the same as the last time she'd seen him, although the light was slowly eking away behind them, dusk or something. "I did go home. I went home. Had a beer, then fell asleep on the sofa."

She glanced around, the reality seeping in. "Oh, okay, a dream. I'm so tired it all seemed to mesh together."

He stopped. They'd reached a wall of rocks stretching out onto the beach, and he perched on one of them, still allowing his feet to dangle in the surging water. "This is a nice place to recharge. I was thinking about the beach before I fell asleep."

"And here we are," she laughed softly. It did feel like energy around her, but she still wanted to lie down and drift away.

"You really need to rest, you know. All of this took so much out of you."

"I know. I just don't know what to do now. It all feels—"

"Different?" he answered.

"Yes, I suppose that's it. Different."

She closed her eyes, feeling the sea spray softly dampen her face and hearing music in the distance. Then it moved closer.

She opened her eyes to the sound of her cell phone serenading her to Fleetwood Mac's *Gypsy* on her nightstand.

"Hello," she answered groggily.

"Where are you?" It took several beats before coherence trickled in.

"Mom?"

"Caroline, you said you'd call me later." She glanced at the Big Ben clock on her night table. It was seven in the evening. She'd been asleep four hours.

"Oh, I'm sorry. I got home and was so tired I just went to bed."

"I'm coming over." The voice was stern and steely, not a combination she appreciated from her mother at this moment.

"No, don't. I'm going to get a shower and then go back to bed. I'll come over tomorrow."

"For breakfast?" Evidently, this was non-negotiable, and she wasn't in the mood to argue.

"Okay, I'll be there."

"Good," sounded like the ice had thawed ever so slightly. "Well, get some rest."

"Okay." She hung up, wondering exactly what she would tell her mom in the morning.

CASSIE BRESLIN

9

Cassie Breslin eyed her daughter with serene, sky-blue eyes as they sipped coffee in the sunroom of her Prytania Street house.

"Are you sure you had enough to eat?"

Caroline looked up at her, her eyes a bit reddened, circles beneath. They betrayed a restless night, although she had assured her mom that this had not been the case. "No, no, I'm fine."

"All you had was one biscuit."

"I don't usually eat a big breakfast."

Cassie sipped her coffee, staring out the window, while Caroline struggled to rid herself of a headache that seemed determined to plague her since she'd awakened. They hadn't spoken about the events of yesterday. Her mother hadn't broached the subject, and Caroline hadn't desired to bring it up.

As it went, Cassie was a relatively young mom—not yet even fifty. She and Caroline's father had married right out of college, and it had been nearly six years since he passed away.

"Have you ever thought about dating again?"

Her mom looked at her with surprise in her calm eyes. "Dating?"

"Yeah, you could, you know. Anyone would be lucky to have you."

"Anyone? Well, first off, my dearest, I wouldn't be looking for anyone. Relationships are complicated and so much more taxing than people acknowledge. People take them so casually, but they have the power to remake your soul or destroy it." She added that part casually as though it were an afterthought.

"What about Dad?"

Cassie sighed deeply. Perhaps Caroline shouldn't have asked, but she was used to her mother being perfectly candid. It was her way.

"I learned a lot in my marriage with your father. I grew a lot, but it wasn't always easy. I guess you could say we weren't on the same path, although I always believed him to be a good man."

"Do you think you shouldn't have married him?"

She hesitated a moment as though considering. "No, as I said, I grew, I learned. If you learn from any experience, it isn't a waste."

Caroline sipped her coffee. It was helping her head. "So, you didn't answer me. Would you date again?"

Cassie smiled. Her eyes narrowed a bit, and Caroline knew that as a signal that she was picking up on something. "Let's see. It really depends on the person. I don't like to waste my time."

Caroline nodded, thinking of Max. She wondered if he'd ever date again after losing his wife—wondered if for him too it depended on the person. She sipped her coffee, relaxing within the thick web of positive energy that always seemed to cocoon her mother's house.

"So," Cassie began casually. Caroline could feel it on the back of her neck. It was coming. Her mother had been polite long enough. "You seemed, I don't know, very odd yesterday."

"It was an odd day," she murmured. She'd thought about it all morning, getting dressed, showering, driving over — thinking, considering how much she was willing to share. And unexpectedly, she was reticent to be too candid. She loved her mother dearly and her aunt as well. But what she didn't want now was too much advice and discussion while she was still in such inner turmoil, still sorting things out.

Her mother remained silent, clearly waiting for her to fill in the blanks. However, that question remained hanging in the air exactly what and how many blanks she was willing to fill in.

"I met someone yesterday."

Cassie leaned back in her chair, bringing the rose-colored coffee cup to her lips. It was a distinctly feminine piece of china. Strangely when she was younger, she didn't remember too many feminine touches in the house. But after her father passed away slowly, Cassie Breslin began to change the atmosphere of the place—first with paintings, dishes, furniture, and then her crowning achievements, the sunroom in the back, and finally, the greenhouse in the backyard. The place granted was in no way overtly feminine, but it had a different aura now, a more sensitive one.

"Really?" was her only comment. She brought the cup back to the table, letting her eyes casually canvass her daughter's face.

"Yes, remember the bookshop?"

"The one on Magazine Street?"

"Yes, Gravier's Bookshop. Well, I met the owner. His name is Max, and he's a widower."

"I see," Cassie commented.

"And," she hesitated, "well, it seems he's a psychic." Her mother was silent, just waiting, quietly waiting. "I think he's the same man I've been seeing in my dreams."

There was a pause, a heavy intense meaning-laden pause, that felt as though it stretched on for hours but in reality, perhaps only lasted a few seconds. "I see," Cassie finally responded. "Well, does he seem to be a nice young man?"

"Um," Good question and a ridiculously difficult question. "I'm not sure. I mean, he was very friendly. I have the feeling he's not over his wife. They seemed close." She picked up her coffee cup and sipped the now tepid liquid.

Cassie eyed her intently, making her again feel like that insecure eleven-year-old girl who had a pension for climbing trees that perhaps shouldn't have been climbed. "You like him."

She frowned. "Sure, I like him as a friend. He's very nice."

"That's not what I mean," she said flatly.

"Well, I don't know, like I said—"

"Be careful," she interrupted. "This feels complicated."

She stared into her mother's warm, compassionate eyes and read the truth within them. "I doubt I'll see him again."

"No, I think you're wrong about that."

AUNT ELISE

10

It was a good day, busy with customers streaming in and out of the bookstore, more than making up for yesterday's lost time. Although he wouldn't exactly classify it as lost time, except from a business evaluation. And truthfully, this was exactly what he needed to clear his mind after a night filled with disturbing and often incoherent dreams. He just needed to throw himself into the mundaneness of retail life and concentrate on worldly concrete matters like unpacking boxes or dusting bookshelves.

About six or seven customers were milling around the store as he sat behind the desk at the register, slowly unpacking a box of inventory. The chime on the door sounded off, and he glanced up. Another woman was entering this time. He could see her clearly. The lady in question wore a rather large floppy hat, sunglasses, and a long paisley-looking skirt with a flowing silky shirt over it. He smiled at her as she crossed in front of the desk that he sat behind. She glanced toward him briefly or as far as he could tell. She hadn't removed the sunglasses, although the bookstore was not brightly lit. Offering him a quick nod, she then continued toward the shelves of books.

He glanced back down at an old volume he'd been inspecting, but Max felt a curious tug at the back of his neck, causing his eyes to rise again. It was his latest customer. It was the woman, now at the other end of the long room, with a book in her hand that she was flipping through. But he felt it again, stronger, emanating from her. She wasn't focused on the book. She was focused on him. He could feel it, in fact, all over his skin. She was canvassing him. He closed his eyes and tried to pinpoint the source of this inquiry. Then he opened them again slowly with understanding.

Standing up from behind the desk, Max walked directly over to the woman stopping in front of her and extending his hand. "Hello, I'd like to introduce myself. I am Max Gravier."

She looked at him with evident surprise, delicately replacing the book on the shelf, then smoothly taking off her sunglasses. She was, he would estimate, in her middle to late forties and had enormous green eyes reminding him of someone in particular. After slightly hesitating, she grasped his hand rather assuredly for a woman, he thought. "I'm Elise, Elise Ashford."

"Ah, good to meet you." There was tremendous energy in her clasp, although she removed her hand rather quickly. "I might be mistaken, but it is just my feeling that you are here for a purpose."

She frowned a bit. She was an extremely attractive woman, although her features were a bit sharp and dramatic, not as soft as. "You are perceptive Mr. Gravier. My niece is—"

"Caroline Breslin," he finished the thought for her.

There was another sort of smile that really wanted to be a frown. "Yes, you are correct, and I am indeed here for a reason, although I am enjoying your lovely establishment."

She seemed a charming woman, silky smooth at moments but also direct and to the point. He tried to appear pleasing, and a part of him was extremely curious. A family where psychic inclinations ran through multiple members was more than intriguing. "Well, is there something specific I can help you with?"

She tilted her head a bit as though considering. "Yes, as a matter of fact, my sister, Caroline's mother, would very much like to invite you to a dinner, a family dinner, at her home this evening."

He looked at her a little blankly. Now, this he hadn't expected. "A dinner?"

She smiled, "Yes, she has a house on Prytania Street and is interested in getting to know you."

"Really?" he asked, still confused.

Her dark green eyes narrowed just a tad. Evidently, he wasn't giving quite the correct response. "Cassie, my sister, understands that you've been very helpful to Caroline, and she would like to meet you."

"So, she sent you to issue this invitation?"

The frown was back. "I volunteered. I was planning to be in the area today."

Something didn't quite hit right, but he rolled with it. "I see."

"If you want to decline Mr. Gravier, I will—"

"No, no, sorry, you just caught me a bit off guard. It sounds very interesting."

She opened her small black purse and took out a business card. "I'll write the address on the back if you have a pen."

He nodded, walking back to his desk and feeling rather than knowing she was right on his heels. Picking up the pen, he spun around and handed it to Elise Ashford. Smoothly she grasped it and scribbled down the required information. "Shall we say around 6:00 or six-thirty?"

It felt remarkably awkward now, the whole situation. "I close at six, so probably the latter."

"Very good, we'll see you then," she answered with a quick smile. And then she returned the sunglasses to her face and made an abrupt exit. So much for enjoying his establishment, he smiled. How very odd. But it did promise to be an eventful evening.

◆

"You did what?" Ever since Caroline had left her mother's house this morning, she had been dragging around the apartment with a slight headache and a desire to sleep for a week. But this, this was unbelievable.

"You don't have to come, dear," her mother's voice was flat, and Caroline detected a tad of irritation.

"So, you and Jared and Aunt Elise can have a lovely dinner with Maximilian Gravier without me?"

There was a quiet hesitation on the other end of the line. "That might be awkward."

"You think? Maybe this whole idea is bordering on being awkward."

"Well, I'll admit it wasn't what I planned. It was more a spur-of-the-moment idea, actually Elise's idea."

Her head was beginning to flare up again. She didn't need this after yesterday's encounter with the Delia creature. She was utterly spent. "And how exactly did this happen?"

"Um, well, you didn't tell me he was psychic."

"I didn't? Wait a minute. Yes, I did."

"You didn't tell me how psychic he was. Elise was, well, just going to check him out."

"What! Am I five?"

"No, of course not, but you are very special and a bit vulnerable, and well, we were curious."

Calm down, calm down. Anger doesn't help the headache. "And then what happened?"

"Well, your aunt went to the bookstore. What did you call it?"

"Gravier's Bookshop."

"Yes, right, and she was just going to slip in and out, you know inconspicuously."

Caroline thought about her spinster aunt and her flair for the dramatic. Inconspicuous was not in her repertoire. "And how did that work out?"

"Um, not well."

"No kidding."

"Yes, it seems your Mr. Gravier isn't just psychic but extremely psychic. He rather quickly picked up on what she was doing."

Her stomach sunk a bit lower. How embarrassing. "I see."

"She had to cover."

"So, she invited him to dinner?"

"She pretended that was her intent all along. She's really great on her feet. So, it will be nice. I'll make jambalaya. He's not allergic to seafood, is he?"

She thought back to their lunch together, two shrimp po'boys. "It doesn't seem so."

"Look, don't worry. We'll keep it light. It might be quite nice." She was silent, having no idea how to respond. "Caroline, are you still there?"

"I think so."

"Between six and six thirty."

"Okay," she murmured begrudgingly.

"Oh, and bring a dessert. Nothing chocolate, Jared hates—"

"Yes, he hates chocolate, got it."

She clicked off the cell phone that she wished dearly she could throw across the room. But just now, after paying all the bills last week, she was tapped out and didn't need the expense of replacing it. She slumped into her sofa, wondering exactly how she would deal with this situation. She'd actually told her mother very little of what had occurred yesterday, but he didn't know that. Wonderful, she had to head off a potential catastrophe. She rooted around on the end table for the card he'd left with her, telling her to call him if needed. Picking up her cell phone, she started to dial, having no earthly idea what she would say or how to make it sound less than mortifying.

"Hello," she hesitated. Maybe she should have thought this through. "Hello."

"Max," she began with no finesse.

"Caroline, what a pleasant surprise."

"Is it really that much of a surprise?"

"No," he sounded amused. How great was that? "I sort of expected to hear from you sometime today."

"Yeah, well, that's just it."

"I saw your aunt today. She invited me to dinner at your mother's house."

Could she melt into the couch and then into oblivion? Didn't seem to be plausible right at the moment, "Um, yeah, about that."

"I was surprised."

"Me too."

"I don't know. I got the feeling she was here for a different reason."

"Yes, with Aunt Elise, it's sort of hard to call."

"So, will you be there?"

"It looks that way. Max, actually the reason I phoned, my family, well, they don't really know about what happened yesterday, except I mentioned I met you. I'm just not ready to bring them in on this."

There seemed to be a hesitation. "Okay, that's fine."

He certainly was making this easy and, in doing that, not making it easy. "Well, are you sure this is okay with you? I mean the dinner thing."

"Are you all right?"

Now that was unexpected. Here she was, tap dancing, and he was concerned about her. "Yes, just tired and headachy, and, well, this kind of caught me off-guard."

"Would you like me to cancel?"

Would she? Good question. "No, not unless you want to."

Another pause, he was thinking it over. She could feel it. And he could probably feel her feeling it, so complicated. "Tell you what, how about I come to pick you up after I close the store? I'll aim for around six. Then that will give us a few moments to regroup before we get to your mother's house."

"Okay, if you want to."

"I think so, and Caroline, one more thing."

"What?"

"Just relax."

She drew a deep breath. "Okay, I'll try."

EVOLVING

11

Just after six, he pulled up on the side of the street, parking near Caroline Breslin's apartment. Stepping out of his car, he found it surprising that he was back here so soon. When he'd left yesterday, he had no intention of seeing her again, at least for a while, at least until certain confusing feelings settled down. But there seemed no time for that. It felt as though he were on a fast train to parts unknown. In fact, it had felt that way a bit since he'd walked into the Milton Latter Library yesterday morning.

Max had contemplated playing it safe, canceling out on the dinner, and resuming life. But something pushed him not to, perhaps a restlessness, perhaps a fatigue of cocooning himself into a half-existence. Also, he was curious, curious about this oddly gifted family. And truth be told, he enjoyed the company of the lovely Ms. Breslin, even enjoying playing the knight who protected her from, well, whatever she needed protecting from.

He ascended the short steps that led into her apartment complex and walked past a small New Orleans-style courtyard at its center. He hesitated near the fountain for a moment, feeling something unusual. Looking upward, he noticed an open doorway in one of the second-floor units. He recognized the eyes immediately, the dark wide, fearful eyes watching him. For a fleeting second, there was recognition, and then in the next moment, Delia quietly closed the door. It left him uneasy, unconvinced that she was back on a good path now.

Clearing his mind, he knocked firmly on Caroline's door. She opened it looking quite entrancing, wearing a long, short-sleeved sweater over an electric blue skirt. But it was immediately her eyes that he focused on, seeming a bit anxious. "You look wonderful," he said.

"Oh, thanks, you too," she replied with distraction.

He waited for a moment. "Can I come in?" he asked a tad awkwardly.

She smiled hesitantly, stepping back as he walked inside. But he didn't like what he was feeling. She was entirely too nervous for it just to be this evening. Caroline closed the door behind him once he was inside. "I'm sorry. I forgot that I need to pick up a dessert," she rambled, not meeting his eyes.

"Are you all right?" he asked directly.

She stilled, finally bringing her gaze up to his. "I don't know. I'm feeling panicked for some reason."

Max reached out, grasping her hand in his. He could feel it—a strange energy, clearly close to an anxiety attack. But it didn't feel like Caroline. It was something else. "This isn't good. You're picking up someone else's feelings."

She shook her head with confusion. "No, no, I can tell when I'm doing that. I just feel—I don't know, like I'm jumping out of my skin."

"Yeah, I can see that. Why don't you get your things, and we'll get out of here?"

"I don't know. I don't know if I can do this tonight." Gently he grasped her arms with his hands firmly, just to get her to focus on him.

"Caroline, you need to get out of here. Right now, that's all. We'll see how you feel after that."

She hesitated but then finally acquiesced. "Okay, I'll get my purse."

He watched her disappear into the bedroom. He was getting impressions, impressions that things were becoming much more complicated than he'd originally thought.

♦

It was bizarre, a distinct impression that she couldn't catch her breath. Max was driving, driving somewhere, but all she could do was close her eyes. "You might want to call your mother and tell her we'll be running late."

"Are we running late?"

He patted her hand reassuringly. "Yes," he answered.

She pulled her cell phone out of her purse, suddenly realizing that she couldn't possibly talk to her mother. She would know, would know that something wasn't right. "I'll text her."

And she clumsily fumbled across her phone to do just that. *Max is picking me up, but we're running a little late.*

"I have to get a dessert."

"I remember," he said. "Any better?"

Her heart seemed to be slowing its breathtaking pace, finally. "I, I think so. I don't know what's wrong with me."

He pulled the car over to a spot on the banks of Bayou St. John. She recognized the tranquil area flanked by beautiful old homes on the side of the water. "What are we doing?" she murmured.

"You're catching your breath."

She nodded. It was so tranquil. Her eyes drifted to the huge metal walking bridge stretching across the water. That's what she would like to do now, forget everything and meander across it. "I don't understand."

"I have an idea," he said quietly.

She smiled. He was a strange man in many ways, sometimes unsettlingly direct and at others so unreadable, opaque. There were so many conflicting impressions that she had of him. "Care to share?"

"I'm coming to suspect that your experience with the creature in the apartment triggered something in you. Basically, that your abilities are evolving."

"That doesn't sound like a bad thing."

"No, no, it doesn't. But it might mean that you're vulnerable for a while until things settle."

She stared at him with confusion. "Vulnerable?"

He nodded, "You might need to take extra care, so you're not bombarded with other people's energy, problems, situations."

She sighed deeply, "I don't need this right now. I can't deal with much more."

He eyed her strangely, "Yes, well, life doesn't usually wait to throw you a curve when you're ready. Usually, it's when you're not."

"I'm sorry," she murmured, connecting to the shift in his mood.

"Sorry for what?" he asked.

"You're talking about your wife and everything that happened. I'm sorry. I feel like I'm intruding somehow with all my craziness."

He laughed softly, "I wouldn't be here if I didn't want to be. And you're certainly not intruding. My wife died over three years ago. Feeling any better now?"

"Yes, calmer. You think I was picking up on someone else."

"I think you have to be careful right now. It's too easy to confuse your sensitivity to others for your emotions. Things need to settle down."

"That's funny. I've been waiting for things to settle down my whole life."

"You're very gifted, Caroline. You just have to find a balance."

"Have you?" she asked impulsively. "Found that balance?"

He smiled, and again she was struck at how handsome he was. She could just collapse into those strong, comforting arms. And she dearly hoped he wasn't reading her thoughts just now. "It's an ongoing process."

She nodded, "So what do you like for dessert that's not chocolate? My brother hates chocolate."

"Well, that rules out a lot."

She laughed, "Yes, a whole universe of options."

◆

"I'm sure it will be fine."

"Are you? I'm not at all certain this is a good idea."

"Well, it wasn't my intention. It was the only thing I could think of on the spur of the moment."

"Yes, well, Caroline is more fragile than we think."

"She's a tank. What's for dinner?"

Cassandra stared at her youngest child in dismay, who had somewhat soundlessly crept into the kitchen behind her and Elise. "Jambalaya, shrimp, and sausage jambalaya." Jared nodded with little expression. He was a young eighteen, his first year in college. Blond like his father, and also unfortunately, at times obtuse like his father was. "Now, Jared, you know that's not true."

"We're not having jambalaya?"

"Your sister is not a tank. She's at a very vulnerable time in her life."

"Is that why you and Aunt Elise are trying to interfere in it?"

She looked at him coolly while Elise couldn't erase a grin that had drifted to her face. "Now, that is unfair. We're just doing this—"

"Because Aunt Elise was spying on this guy, and she got caught. You need to work on that Auntie. More stealth," he commented as he walked out the kitchen.

Elise couldn't help it. She burst out laughing. "That boy is a handful, Cassie. Maybe I should go. This might be awkward."

Cassie put the top back on the pot of simmering jambalaya and glared at her younger sister. "Really? Awkward?"

Elise smiled at her sheepishly. "I'll just go set the table. Shouldn't they be here by now?"

Cassandra glanced at the clock. They were fifteen minutes late, but then again Caroline had told her they were running late. Her stomach sank. Perhaps, this was a mistake. Perhaps, it was best just to step back completely, even though her acute senses warned her of impending peril. And she wondered for a moment what Allen would have advised. But then again, as she remembered, he'd left all these decisions to her. She pushed away the memory. There was no point in dwelling in painful places that should not impact the present.

The Family Dinner

12

It was a lovely Queen Anne style house that Caroline had directed him toward right on a corner of Prytania Street, a lovely area of the city known as the Garden District. He and Sophie had taken many walks in the area as she took pictures. But that was long before she'd become ill. He stopped the car in the long curving driveway around the side of the house, but Caroline made no move to get out the car. She just sat there, eyes closed.

"Are you all right?" he asked calmly.

"I don't know, a bit of a headache flared up. I'm just a mess today."

Max closed his own eyes and attempted to feel. He was picking up a strange flux of somewhat unstable energy around her, as though an array of things were being drawn to her in her present state. "You know this might not be the best night for this. You may need to rest."

She shook her head. "No, it will be all right. I always feel better when my family is around me. It helps me feel stronger at times." He understood, again energy.

"All right, but if you start feeling unwell let me know. We can leave."

She turned to him smiling. "You're so gallant Mr. Gravier." And it struck him strangely, almost like a déjà vu that he couldn't place.

"Not always so noble C—" and then he stopped. He'd almost called her something else, as though it was familiar. "Maybe we should go in now before your family begins to wonder what's going on."

She nodded, finally stepping out of the car with the cheese-cake she'd been holding.

♦

It was an unusual vibration that hit him as he crossed the threshold of Cassandra Breslin's Prytania Street address. The first sensation that struck him acutely was energy. It was more than clear to him that Caroline's family was no ordinary group of individuals. The second feeling that hit him quite unexpectedly was one of familiarity, as though he had spent a bit of time here before or perhaps would someday.

Caroline hugged the ash-blond woman moments after she'd walked in, and then glanced over to him looking a bit ill at ease. Of course, this was a bit strange for her, should be for him too, but he was enjoying the distraction too much. "Mom this is Max, Maximilian Gravier," she murmured.

Her mother smiled graciously, clearly an elegant lady holding out her hand to him. "Good to meet you Mr. Gravier. I'm Cassie Breslin."

He grasped her hand and again sensed the strong psychic energy that evidently ran through this family. "Please call me Max, and I do appreciate the kind invitation this evening."

She smiled again and nodded, "Of course, I hope you like jambalaya." And then she gestured behind her to the tall young man and petite dark-haired woman who had been hanging a bit further back. "I'd like you to meet my son Jared, and I think you already know my sister."

◆

It should have been awkward. And it was, but then it wasn't because of Max. Max seemed to fit right in. And for her family that was more than unusual. It wasn't that most people acted oddly toward them. It was that they seemed uncomfortable with most people, although they acted as though they didn't.

But Max laughed at Jared's jokes, talked a bit about his bookstore, listened to Aunt Elise's theories about the paranormal hot spots in the city, and complemented her mother's food sincerely.

Then they'd adjourned to one of her mother's favorite spots—the sunroom at the back of the house for coffee and dessert, her cheesecake, where they watched the night finally envelop everything. It had gone well, unbelievably well. But for her something still was off. She felt as though it was building inside her skin, something that no one could see, nor understand, something that was driving her quite nuts.

"Are you all right Caroline?" her mother asked. "You look pale."

She'd smiled, "Just tired. A headache, it's been a long day."

She felt Max's eyes on her. In fact, she'd felt them keenly all evening, but she didn't meet them. He was too perceptive, and she didn't want that just now. She just wanted to hide somewhere, to sleep and fix whatever was going crazy inside of her. "Are you sure that's all it is Cara?" Cassandra murmured to her.

She smiled again trying to fake pleasantness. "Of course, I'm sure this coffee will help," she said sitting down on the end of a rattan loveseat on the porch. She was concentrating on trying to clear her mind, trying to find stillness while conversation continued around her. She could hear Jared and Aunt Elise's voice discussing constellations that her aunt pointed out through the great plate glass window in her mother's sunroom. Then her mother excused herself from the room momentarily. And Max, Max sitting down beside her on the couch and putting his coffee and cheesecake on the small glass table in front of them. "Do you want me to take you home?" he asked quietly.

Her eyes flickered open. She hadn't realized they'd been closed. But he did look serious now, not the relaxed jovial self he'd been through most of the evening.

"Why, do I look that bad?" she asked.

He nodded a bit gravely, "Not the best. I'm worried about you. What is it exactly?"

"I don't know. I just feel—" and she floundered for words that she couldn't grasp. Then he reached out and took her hand. And that silenced her mumbling.

It was steadying. His contact to her was always calming. "Finish your coffee. We need to get going," he whispered.

She nodded. What else could she do? Then she noticed her mother had walked back into the room, and her eyes were on them both.

◆

"What do you think?" she asked her sister as they sat outside on the porch glider watching the last vestiges of the day's light just slip away.

Elise glanced up. Eyes dark with contemplation, Cassie thought.

73

"About?" she asked softly.

Cassie frowned, sharply nudging her sister in the side. "What do you think of Maximilian Gravier?"

"Seems like a nice enough fellow," she murmured. Not willing it seemed to elaborate on much of anything.

"Yes," echoed Cassie, "seems nice I suppose."

Elise laughed a bit softly, "But—" she added with emphasis.

"Well, I don't know. Caroline seems to like him. I think. I mean I could feel—"

"Chemistry," Elise offered.

"Well, I don't know, maybe. Do you think it was chemistry?"

"It crackled," she said blandly.

"Oh, I don't know if that's good. He's a widower, probably still in love with well—"

"His dead wife?"

"Elise that is very crass of you. I mean, well yes, I'm sure his emotions are still tied up with well—"

"His dead wife."

"Would you please stop saying that? It's very disrespectful."

"Is it more respectful to say his deceased wife?"

"I don't know. I just don't want Cara getting tied up with someone who is committed elsewhere."

"I don't know if you could call him committed. I mean she's not a viable option anymore."

"Elise, good lord, can you just—"

"Anyway, it's too late."

Cassie straightened up a bit from against the swing. "What do you mean too late?"

"I mean they're sharing secrets. Couldn't you see the looks exchanged, furtive mysterious glances? They're hiding something."

"Do you think they're involved?"

Elise shrugged her small sharp shoulders a bit. "In what respect?"

THE SCARF

13

"Do you want to go for a drive by the lakefront?" She glanced up, a bit surprised at the question. She'd assumed that after her mother's dinner party, Max would be inclined to take her straight home. "I thought the energy from the water might help revive you."

"Sure, that would be nice," she answered.

She let her head, which was still pounding a bit, lie back against his car's headrest. It was dark. The sky was only illuminated by stars and what her aunt would call a waxing gibbous moon. "I can't remember what it means, the waxing moon," she commented almost to herself.

"Let's see. The first quarter moon, if I remember, is the time of caution."

"That's right," she murmured, staring out into the darkness of the sky. "Walking the knife's edge between dark and light."

"That sounds very dramatic."

"Well, yes, that's my aunt. But the point is balance, choices, new doorways."

"Hmm, new doorways?"

"Yes," she murmured, staring out into the night. Even with the occasional streetlamp, it was almost too dark to see the water. But she could sense it, feel the power of it.

"Are you feeling any better?" he asked.

"A bit, thank you. I'm sorry to have dragged you into all of this. I mean with my family. They're very protective of me, clannish, I suppose."

"It's clear how much they care about you. After all, they sent your Aunt Elise on reconnaissance."

"No, I imagine she volunteered. She lives for that sort of thing."

He laughed, "That sounds a bit sarcastic."

She turned to him with little expression. "Does it? Sorry, I was being perfectly serious. She's quite eccentric, very sharp, but a bit nutty."

"That's not always a bad thing in this world to be eccentric."

She sighed in a way that left him wondering what was behind it. "Now that sounds jaded."

"No, I just meant it helps to have some protection, whatever that looks like. That seems to be your problem just now. No protection, in a psychic sense, I mean."

She closed her eyes, "Is that what you've been doing, Max? Protecting me?" He didn't answer. He wasn't sure what he was doing here with her, not at all."

◆

He'd decided to take Caroline Breslin home, though oddly enough, he didn't want to. He was enjoying the evening, had enjoyed the dinner with her family but was enjoying the time alone with her even more. And he felt guilty about it, although exactly why he couldn't pinpoint. Saying it was Chloe was an easy answer but one that didn't quite suffice—if he were to be honest. He'd intended this to be the end of his association with Caroline, this dinner, this unexpected dinner he'd sort of been roped into but had enjoyed immensely. He liked her family, but the truth was that he liked watching her interacting with her family — the easy give and take, the nuances between them. It made him feel a bit lonely. It was true that he'd cut himself off after Chloe's death, deliberately, surgically. But now it felt hollow. And he, well, he needed more.

He stopped the car in front of her apartment complex. And waited, waited for an extended moment. She'd made no move to get out of the car.

"Are you all right?" he asked. Her eyes were staring forward, just glued to the building.

"Do you want to come in?" she asked rather quickly.

"Well," he began, a bit surprised.

"No, no, I'm sorry. I guess that sounded like. Well, I don't know. I'm nervous about going in there tonight. It feels creepy, and I thought if you came in just for a little while, it might chase anything away that shouldn't be there—" her voice sort of rambled down into a barely audible tone.

"Of course," he answered smoothly, reaching over and squeezing her hand. It was a contact that he'd meant as reassuring but felt more electric than he'd anticipated because there was this attraction, hard to deny.

She looked up into his face with a tentative smile that made him feel as though she were very vulnerable. "Thank you, Max." Yes, Max, where had all your good intentions gone? Where indeed?

◆

It was like nightmares, when she'd wake up in the middle of the night after a scary dream and find herself alone in her apartment. That was perhaps the hardest part of living alone. In her time living here, it had happened more than once. Sometimes when she woke up with the dread still drenching her, she'd stay awake for hours, watching TV, until the dream's clinging aura was finally chased out of her conscious mind. And now, not unlike the aftermath of a nightmare, the prospect of walking into her empty apartment all alone tonight seemed unbearable. So, she'd invited Max to come inside. She wondered if she should offer him a nightcap or if he thought this was some kind of a proposition. And if that would be such a terrible thing? Of course, it would be a first for her, inviting a man in for a nightcap or anything else.

They'd meandered into the den. Out of habit, she'd dropped her purse on the coffee table, realizing this wasn't the tidiest thing to do in front of company. But then again, she rarely had company except for her family.

She turned on her heel smiling at him. "Would you like a drink? Uh, I mean, something to drink? I could make tea, you know, herbal tea or something, or coffee, but we had that at Mom's."

He stood there smiling down at her because he was a bit taller, seeming the tiniest bit bewildered. "Are you all right, Caroline?"

"Oh yes, just a little spacey. So much has been happening. Believe it or not, my life isn't usually this eventful."

He nodded slowly, "Tea would be fine."

"Okay, have a seat, and I'll get it." And then she headed toward the kitchen. Good lord, have a seat. How awkward. He'd probably drink his tea and run for the hills. As she reached the small galley kitchen, she instinctively grabbed the counter for balance. Another peculiar wave of dizziness had hit her. She breathed deeply, trying to get hold of herself. Maybe she was just getting sick. But as she reached into the cabinet for the box of tea bags, she knew deep down that there was more to this.

◆

Max didn't sit, not for a moment. He started wandering, wandering with a purpose, through Caroline's apartment. Something was definitely not right here. She'd felt it, perhaps not even consciously, and that was why she'd invited him in. He allowed his senses to expand, feeling vibrations around him. There was a pull. He felt a distinct pull into her bedroom.

Slowly, he opened the door of the darkened room, allowing it to swing open. It wasn't the same as before with Delia's creature. But there was something here. It seemed icy to him, although he knew without question that the temperature was no cooler than in the rest of the apartment. No, definitely, he was picking up on something less obvious, something different.

He flicked on the light switch by the door, cautiously looking around. Nothing, in particular, appeared amiss in the room. Some clothing was thrown in disarray on the bed. He could feel Caroline trying to decide what to wear. She'd been nervous. He breathed deeply, feeling it again—an agitation, being exhausted, drained. But it was subtle, subtle enough for her not to be able to pinpoint it.

He walked further into the room, the chill again, coldness emanating from something. He let himself feel, although it was difficult, like a grating against his nerves. He reached out his hand, sensing a pull toward the large, cherry wood dresser against the wall. Both hands now brushed along its smooth surface until they stopped as though they'd met an impediment—right at the drawer, second to last from the bottom.

Max didn't consider if this was an intrusion. Instead, he just allowed his instincts to take hold. Opening the drawer, he could feel Caroline's energy permeating the clothing. But there was something else that he could also feel, like an irritation creeping up his hands. He dug deeply through a stack of shirts until he reached the bottom surface of the drawer. His hands spread out, spanning the rough wooden surface until they hit it — icy, sharply chilling. With effort, he grabbed the source of the painful sensation and yanked it out, a scarf, a strange red and black scarf. He straightened up, examining it closely with his hands.

"What are you doing?" It surprised him. In fact, he nearly jumped, having been so engrossed in his quest. He turned to Caroline, standing in the doorway with two steaming cups of tea in her hands, looking slightly shocked. And it occurred to him, perhaps for the first time, that this must look more than a bit strange. So, in explanation, he held out the scarf toward her. Almost immediately, her expression changed, her eyes focusing on it as though trying to fix on something.

"Where did you get that?" she asked with confusion.

"In your dresser."

"But it's not mine," her eyes narrowed a bit. "I remember seeing Delia wearing that."

He looked down at the scarf. It was nothing particularly special on the surface, just a light, silky scarf that felt like icy fire in his hands. It was clear to him that some sort of ceremony had been performed on this thing before it was planted in Caroline's apartment.

She walked closer, standing beside him. "What do you think it means?"

"Your friend Delia has been in this apartment, I take it," he murmured.

"Well yeah, a few times, not often. Once her plumbing was messed up, and she used the bathroom."

"The one off this bedroom?"

"Yes," she said, swallowing on a dry throat. "It's the only one, such a small place. What do we do with it? Throw it away, return it?"

"Not yet. Maybe just try to get some answers from it." And then he looked up at her as though trying to refocus. "Can I have my tea now?"

Her brow wrinkled a bit. "I guess so if you still want it."

THE RED-HAIRED WOMAN

14

Thank the heavens, tomorrow was Sunday. It was approaching ten, an hour when she was usually in bed if she worked the next day. She and Max sat on her short sofa staring at the red and black scarf that lay crumpled up on her coffee table. It was the table that Jared had constructed out of pine in a furniture design class in his first semester at college. He'd dropped the class, but she'd gotten the table.

She took another sip of her now less-than-steamy blueberry tea. "Do you like the tea?" she asked. Max was sitting near her, hard not to, on her very short and cozy little green couch. But he hadn't spoken much. He just seemed utterly absorbed in focusing on Delia's crushed-up ugly scarf. Kind of hideous, she thought. It was definitely nothing she would wear.

"Hmm," he responded a bit distantly.

"It's blueberry, supposed to be good for stress. At least that's what Aunt Elise says."

"Do you have a lot of stress?" he asked, although she could feel his mind was far away.

"Judging from the last few days, I'd say yes."

He turned to her with a bit of a somber expression that gave her a few butterflies in the stomach area. "It has been a bit chaotic. And yes, I like the tea," he said, taking a sip, then placing the mug on the coffee table on the little bright, purple coaster she'd placed there in anticipation of a few quiet moments to-gether—before, of course, all the scarf ruckus broke out. "It's clear that Delia's involvement with you isn't as random as it seemed at first glance."

"I know. She's such a bitch," she spurt out rather hotly. "Oh, sorry, I just really don't need this right now, you know. I have too many other things to deal with, like life, my job."

"Yes, well, that is the nature of life. It doesn't wait for you to be ready for much of anything."

Sighing inwardly, how callous and superficial she must sound. She wasn't, really. At least, she didn't think she was. All of it just felt like more than she could handle. He reached out with-out looking at her and patted her hand as in response to her thoughts. "Max, I know it's not fair of me to continually ask for your help. I mean, you have your own life to deal with, but I really don't know what this means. What to do about this, if it means anything."

"She's used the scarf to get to you, placing it in your bedroom where frankly, you are vulnerable. You sleep. You change clothes. It's almost as though you had a psychic voyeur just watching you."

It took a moment for his words to seep in, but they did. But all it served to do was shoot white hot fire through her veins. Again, he squeezed her hand. "That won't help now, Caroline. You have to have a clear mind. We need to focus."

"Focus how?"

"Another exploration, I'm afraid. But we start now with the scarf and follow its trail."

◆

Getting into the proper frame of mind for a meditation with the scarf in such close proximity was difficult. There was a keenly disruptive, negative energy emanating from it. And clearly, it had affected Caroline, eroded her in some respects. At another time, when she was on a more solid footing, it might not have bothered her. But she was in a transient period of growth with respect to her psychic inclinations that somehow left her quite unprotected.

Caroline was settling beside him on the carpet in front of the sofa. They'd moved the coffee table and placed the scarf on a white pillowcase she had dug out of her linen closet. "You know, I've met several Wiccans. Aunt Elise has even dabbled in it."

"Yes, there is nothing problematic about the philosophy, but anything can be abused. Wiccan teaching might start as the base but whatever Delia is dabbling in has moved into a much darker area. Are you ready?"

She was sitting next to him cross-legged as they had meditated together in his shop the day before. He could feel the warring energies all over her, something struggling to attach itself to her and drain her, he assumed. "It's difficult even to be calm," she answered.

"I know. Just do your best to maintain a white light around you, protecting you." She nodded, closing her eyes and concentrating. Again, he was struck by her beauty, not so much of the physical kind, although there was that, but a glow that she had about her, an aura of purity, dare he say. He wasn't sure it was the best choice to drag her through this in the state she was in, though he knew without question that he didn't want to leave her behind.

He took her hand in his and closed his eyes, allowing himself to be drawn toward the energies of the scarf. "Caroline, I need you to focus on staying with me."

"Yes," she responded softly. He could feel the change in her already, moving somehow beyond the attacking forces around her. It was clear that she was stronger than he'd thought.

He could see the scarf now in his vision, as though it were alive, writhing around on the white pillowcase like a hissing, black and red serpent. *"Commence,"* he commanded in his mind, and the thing moved off the white cotton cloth, beginning to slither across the room.

With his astral body, Max stood and pulled Caroline to her feet.

"Where are we going?" she spoke to his mind.

"Wherever it leads us."

Traveling in meditation is not like walking out of a room. In the manner of thought, one travels. The disturbing thing had crossed through the apartment to the front doorway. Although they were without bodies, with concentration, Max maintained the link with Caroline. More succinctly, in his mind, he was holding onto her hand.

She was quiet, clearly concentrating on remaining with him, while he focused on following the grisly thing. In his experience, everything leaves a trail, whether you can view it in the physical world or not. As it moved within his psychic vision, the twisting serpent seemed to shed little particles of its skin that almost appeared as a path of sizzling ash. It wasn't easy to continue to follow it. Every natural instinct within him was to get as far away from the repellant thing as possible. It was made of low, coarse matter found in the basest creations. People had no clue the damage that fooling around with this sort of low-level matter could cause not to others but themselves.

This sort of base, negative manifestation just didn't go away. It clung to you, tried to mesh, incorporate itself into your energy, your very make-up as a human being. It is not easy to rid yourself of such an entity once you've committed your own energies to it.

But in this, he had no choice but to follow. They continued to track it through Caroline's doorway to outside below within the ground-level courtyard. As they stood near the central fountain, the sky overhead was clouded with its half-moon semi-shrouded in the muffled darkness.

"What now?" he could hear Caroline whisper into his mind.

He focused his energy on the wriggling thing that now seemed to hiss and to steam from the exposed parts of its body that had shed the skin. *"Reveal,"* he murmured on a level that could reach the manifestation.

Overhead the sky began to mutate, the illumination around them increasing, reaching a level that appeared close to dusk. Delia suddenly appeared before them, near the fountain, dressed in a long black skirt and short-sleeved black top with the infamous scarf tied at her neck. *"Can she see us?"* Caroline beside him asked with some concern.

"No, this is clearly the past."

Then he felt it behind him before he heard it. It was an irritating energy as though a nasty group of insects had suddenly descended. And on its footsteps, almost a shuffling sound as someone approached.

He shook his head nearly in disbelief. So strange, on the surface, it just seemed like an innocuous, older woman, mid-sixties, well-kept, on the petite side, with the only odd characteristic being a rather bold, nearly unnatural shade of bright orange hair. She smiled as she approached Delia, reaching out to touch her with a markedly bony hand.

"Do you know who she is?" he quickly asked Caroline.

He could feel her beside him, but she was silent. *"Caroline!"*

"I'm sorry, something about her. I feel so weak," she managed to get out hesitantly.

"Well, I'm not surprised. After all, it's clear she is the author of all this."

◆

Caroline kept close to Max. It took all her concentration to accomplish this, and it only got worse when that strange little woman greeted Delia. On the surface, no one would know that anything was amiss. She seemed like just a nice little lady, well-groomed as any you would see wandering the stores of Canal Place on any given day.

But beneath, she was all wrong. Caroline felt keenly as though someone had punched her directly in the chest. If she indeed still had a chest in this form that they were traveling in. Even in their astral state, she felt Max squeeze her hand. It made her feel stronger. He was giving her energy. She was certain, but to do that, he had to be depleting himself.

"Max!"

"Ssssshhhhh, they're moving."

And as she found, so were they. They followed the pair through one of the front doors of an upper apartment she knew belonged to Delia.

As they crossed the threshold, she realized dimly that she'd never physically stepped foot in Delia's apartment. Except, of course, for that little foray, they took into it astrally to confront her about the horrible creature she'd created. Now here, again, they were tracking another horrible creature of hers that used to be neck apparel.

Delia flicked on lights, and for the first time, Caroline noted how sparsely furnished it was. No television, no sofa, some chairs scattered here and there but no artwork. There was a huge wicker trunk against the wall and a small black table with a black candle that looked like — *"Are you kidding me?"* she said to Max. *"An altar?"*

"Seems so."

"No wonder the boyfriend left. I mean, look at this place."

"Probably the deterioration after his departure."

"I don't know about that. I'd say this deterioration has been going on for a while."

The two women had pulled up chairs directly before her macabre little dark altar. And the creepy redhead seemed to be muttering something inaudible to herself. "To achieve what you desire, my child, you must obtain power."

"Power, hierophant?" Delia responded.

"Good grief," Caroline muttered.

"Yes, yes, there is strong energy not far at all from you. And it is right that you should take it, my child."

"Energy from where?"

"The adept who lives above you, the girl with the green eyes."

Caroline gasped, but Max squeezed her hand to warn her to remain calm.

"Caroline, but will it hurt her?"

"Of course not. We true practitioners never really do anything to harm anyone. We simply seek to balance things." Caroline was astonished at the convincing lies that seemed to dribble out of the woman's mouth.

"Yes, yes, I can see that—balance." Delia pounced on, clearly eager to lap up the lies.

"What do we need?" she asked.

The little matronly but now extremely creepy woman looked at her momentarily and then pointed to the scarf around her neck. "We need a focal point. Once I have imbued this possession of yours with purpose, then you will have to plant it in her home. Not just anywhere but where she sleeps."

Delia untied the scarf and put it into the redhead's bony hands. "I'm so grateful. How can I repay you?" she asked.

The woman stretched the scarf tightly. "No matter, things will balance out."

Caroline felt an acute dizziness sweep through her, and then suddenly she was back sitting on the carpet in her apartment. She slumped over a bit, her heart area aching profoundly.

She felt Max's hand on her back. "What happened?" she whispered.

"We've seen enough, and you are very drained."

"What about the scarf?" she asked.

"Now we burn it," he said icily.

THE ATTACK

15

And they did burn the scarf, although it took a while, and scorched up one of her few aluminum pans. But finally, Delia's wretched black and red hideous scarf was in ashes. And Caroline didn't feel much better.

She glanced at the clock she'd hung in her galley kitchen. It was one of those cats whose eyeballs move and tail wags simultaneously—Jared's idea. It was closing in on eleven.

"Is the bookstore open tomorrow?" she murmured.

"Not until one. It's a short day."

"Yeah, hmm, so, do you think this is the end of this business?" She asked but dubiously dreading the answer.

Max was leaning against the counter, sort of staring at the pile of ashes that used to be Delia's scarf. "No, unfortunately, I imagine not."

She frowned despondently. "I had a feeling you might say that."

"Yes, if items were planted in your house, I imagine items were stolen as well. Usually, it is the way this kind of dirty business is conducted."

"I don't know. I just don't understand how I could be vulnerable to this sort of hijinks."

He smiled. She thought at her use of the word hijinks. It was one of Aunt Elise's terms that she'd absorbed without acknowledging it. "Well, all I can say is that it is largely timing. They caught you at a bad time and now have gotten their hooks in, although I suspect Delia is more of a puppet for this other woman."

"The horrid redhead?"

"Yes, she's using Delia and clearly pulling tremendous energy from you."

"What in the world do we do?" she asked him, the universe, herself — just about anything that could offer her some hope that this would all end soon.

Max seemed focused, determined, undaunted, and it helped her to rally her courage. Quite coolly, he replied, "We'll have to track her down. But it will have to wait until tomorrow, I think. It's so late. How about I set up camp on your sofa this evening?"

Caroline looked at him a bit blankly. This was unexpected. "My sofa?"

"It's either that or carting you back to your mother's house. You aren't staying here alone until we get this settled."

"Well," that perhaps more than much of the evening's events did manage to take her breath away. "I'll get some blankets."

She headed back towards the bedroom, wondering what, indeed, was next.

◆

Caroline had lent him a spare toothbrush that, luckily, she'd had on the side. She'd given him sheets, a pillow, and a quilt that felt distinctly as though her mother had a hand in its construction. What he hoped to accomplish here was somewhat beyond him. He couldn't shake the feeling that a threat, a vague, insubstantial threat, loomed over them.

Yes, of course, the destruction of the scarf was positive. But, as he'd told Caroline, it hadn't solved the problem. There were pieces here, intangible pieces that he couldn't quite link together as of yet.

He settled back in the semi-darkness of Caroline's den. She'd left a light on in the kitchen for him before she'd told him good-night. By that time, she was dressed in a grey t-shirt and sweatpants, and he wondered distantly why she seemed so appealing to him—as appealing as if she'd been decked out in a sexy negligee. It was this thing. The thing going on between them was becoming more difficult to hold at bay. He was still a reasonably young man, not immune to the charms of a beautiful woman. Clearly, he was not immune to the charms of this particularly beautiful young woman who, in just a few days, was burrowing beneath his defenses and making the idea of throwing caution to the wind more and more a plausibility.

But first, he had to deal with the crazy girl upstairs and her mentor.

He closed his eyes and allowed his exhausted mind to travel wherever it wished.

Calming images of the ocean rolled over him. It was his solace, the healing energy of water.

Then in the distance, he could hear a familiar voice calling. *"Max, what will you do now?"*

It was like a stab. He allowed himself to be drawn to the hospital room, where Chloe slowly and systematically drifted away from him. It was painful to return here, but he understood that memories often came back as teaching tools. Because of the painful emotion, what was not understood at the moment might be later gleaned in recollection.

"What did you say, my love?"

She was in and out of consciousness, sometimes murmuring things he found completely nonsensical and at other moments crystal clear as though she fully comprehended everything happening. The doctors had assured him there was no pain. That, at the very least, comforted him, although they claimed it was the medication that often caused her lapses of clarity.

"I said, Max, what will you do now?"

His throat went dry at the question. Best to keep things superficial, he'd been told, but another part of him felt differently. He felt that Chloe would be comforted if loose ends were tied up.

"Don't worry about me, my darling."

She spoke softly. "You've always been there to take care of me, Max. I'm sorry there weren't any children to be with you."

"Stop, please stop. Everything's all right."

Her eyes fluttered open. "Promise me that you won't stop living. I'm finished here. Moving on now. But there are things for you to do, and you shouldn't let yourself be alone."

"Chloe, please, just rest."

"Promise me. It will help. Just promise."

"Yes, of course, I promise." He'd forgotten that. It had become so intertwined with all the pain. Of course, he would have promised her the moon at that point. And perhaps he had, anything to bring her peace. He breathed deeply at the memory, a stab still lodged in his heart at the recollection. He did torture himself — the things he didn't do, the things he did, refusing to accept that there was no right way to ease a loved one's passing from this world. You simply did the best you could and prayed fervently for God to do the rest.

He breathed in deeply, concentrating on the sound of the ocean that he could summon easily to soothe him. It was meditative, calming. Then suddenly, his eyes flew open.

He felt it acutely. They were no longer alone.

♦

Caroline dreamed, although, within the dream, she was unaware. She walked barefoot through an old house, decrepit, smelling of damp, rotten wood. She could not understand in any coherent way why she was here—so deep was she caught up in the moment.

She breathed in and felt the stench of mold enter her lungs so much that it gagged her. There was no breath. It felt like panic, like suffocation. Her naked feet scraped splintering wood and got caught on a rusty nail sticking up from the decaying slats of the floorboards.

There was jagged pain as she pulled her foot away, seeing the blood oozing from the wound. Desperately, she searched for a way out. Uneven light trickled in from somewhere, but she couldn't find or reach it.

Then from behind her, a hand covered her mouth, stifling her scream. It covered her, the shadow, the dark shape burying her, suffocating as she struggled desperately for air but was unable to emit any sound. And she thrashed helplessly, to no avail.

♦

As Max entered the bedroom, he saw the darkness barely illuminated by a nightlight from the bathroom. Nothing was here, but he could see Caroline restlessly moving and moaning in her sleep. He focused, making his vision shift so that he began to see.

Just bending over her on the bed was a dark shadow and, around it, a red glow. At first glance, it appeared as some odd amorphous blob of light, but then he could see it solidifying in parts. It seemed to be struggling with Caroline, fighting to pull energy out of her. It was clear to him that the connection they'd broken with the scarf made it more difficult but not impossible.

He focused even more deeply, trying to launch right into the heart of this psychic attack. What he saw was energy, a manifestation but one connected to an individual. Now feeling as though he'd reached a similar transient state, he connected with the figure, yanking it forcibly off Caroline. It fell back against a wall, scattering to the ground. What was solid in it had facial features— fangs and red eyes glowing with its source of negative energy. It was mindless and yet scrambling back to feed on its prey. But again, again, he launched a blow against it, and it focused on him confused with eyes, eyes he recognized. The woman with Delia was guiding it.

Steeling himself with a force he mustered from unknown sources, he launched one more blow splattering the creature to the floor until it dissipated.

He breathed deeply, completely drained, then returned to his body. Caroline had not surfaced from the dream. She continued to moan and thrash about frantically. Now moving toward her, he grasped her arms and shook her softly to awaken her.

Her eyes opened, still caught up in confusion. "It's all right," he murmured soothingly, pulling her against his chest. "It's all right."

His heart was still hammering from the encounter, but he'd felt he'd dealt the woman a blow. She'd taken a lot of risks attacking this way, evidently feeling confident that she would meet with no opposition.

♦

Caroline was breathing deeply, completely confused. She felt like she'd been trapped somewhere in hell and awoken to feel Max holding her tightly, murmuring soothing things into her ear.

His heart was pounding. She could feel it, being held so softly against his chest. But her head was spinning in complete confusion. "What happened?" she stammered.

"An attack, but you're safe. It's all right." She believed him, believed him, and didn't want to move. She felt so safe now, and moments before, it seemed as though she was literally suffocating. "Are you all right?" he whispered into her hair.

She didn't want to say yes, because he might leave. And just now, she didn't want him ever to leave. "I, I think so," she murmured."

Then he pulled away, and the coldness of the world swept in between them. But he was still holding her arms. "Are you sure?" he said.

She continued to breathe deeply. It felt as though she just couldn't get enough air. "I don't know. I was being smothered. Something horrible was suffocating me. Was it a dream?"

His face looked grave but primarily concerned about her. "Partly but mostly a psychic attack."

"That woman?" she asked, more than a bit horrified.

"Yes, but I think she got more than she was looking for."

She looked at him, nodding but then couldn't help it. The tears began to flow. This was simply too much. All the stress of the last few days simply came crashing down on her.

She felt his hand brushing away the tears rolling down her face with abandon. "It's all right, Caroline," he said.

"I'm so tired," she whispered. "All of this. It won't stop."

"It's all right," he repeated, holding her face with both his hands. And then he was closer, so close — leaning in and kissing her softly. She pulled back in surprise. She hadn't expected this, maybe had wanted it but hadn't expected it at all. He seemed frozen, just looking at her intently, but then as though a decision had been made, he leaned in, kissing her again, now clearly with more passion. Passion that she knew she could drown in as he pulled her more closely into his arms.

AN IMPOSSIBLE NIGHT

16

Max couldn't stop himself from kissing her and didn't want to. She needed him, and more than that, he needed her desperately. But he did stop himself from making love to her. That wouldn't be right. She was too vulnerable, awakened from a horrible nightmare/psychic attack. Although she might go along with him in the heat of the moment, he didn't think it was fair to her. No matter how much he might want this.

So, he pulled back, pulled back from a passionate embrace that felt as though it was ready to escalate wildly at any given moment. "Cara," he whispered huskily. He used that name. He'd heard her mother use it, and now he felt it was his to use.

She looked at him, surprised. She looked at him bleary-eyed. She looked at him with a tinge of disappointment. "Yes," she murmured in a voice that only made him want to forget good intentions and let passion take its course.

"We have to stop."

"Oh," she answered again, now with a tangible disappointment that kind of clawed at him. "We do?"

He smiled. This would probably be tougher than slugging the bizarre blob of negative energy that had been attacking her. "I think so. Too much is happening now."

She nodded, still beautifully disheveled. "Yeah, okay." And then she looked around the room a bit fearfully. "I don't know what I'm going to do. I can't sleep in here."

He glanced around. She was right. There was no guarantee that thing wouldn't return. "Yeah, okay, bring a pillow. Let's set up on the couch."

She grabbed a pillow and quickly hopped out of bed. She seemed so young to him now and moments before— Well, in hopes of getting some rest in the night, he pushed those particular images out of his head.

♦

She smiled at him groggily. "Coffee is ready."

It was nearly nine. He knew he had to get home. He knew he had to shower and get ready to open the shop after lunch. But having slept very little the night before, all of that seemed akin to climbing a mountain—difficult and unappealing.

"Oh, that would be great," he muttered, following Caroline into her kitchen. She was still dressed in the t-shirt and sweatpants she'd slept in, if indeed one could call it sleeping.

They'd sat up on the couch for a while, then her leaning against him with a pillow. Later he had his arm around her, and both dozed off, then woke up. Then she'd moved to a chair, trying to curl up, and then her feet on another chair. Feeling guilty, he offered her the couch because, after all, his feet sort of stuck out off it due to his height. Around two, she'd grabbed a pile of blankets off her bed and lay on the floor. Then he pulled cushions off the couch and blankets and ended up on the floor too. And this had been the best solution until he'd woken up with pains and odd creaking noises everywhere in his body.

He picked up the cup of coffee she'd poured, which was completely black, and sipped it. "You don't want milk or sugar?" she asked.

"Probably," he murmured.

She grinned at him a bit too perkily. How exactly that could be after the night they'd had, he didn't know. "So, Max," she smiled a bit. "What's next?"

"You should pack a bag and stay at your mother's house."

The perkiness dimmed a notch. "Do you really think that's necessary?"

He stirred the coffee to which he'd just added milk and a teaspoon of sugar. One sip, yes, that was more familiar. "I do."

"How will I explain it?"

His somewhat blurry vision focused on her face. "Tell them the truth."

There was rather a protracted pause. "If I do that, they'll never let me set foot back here."

"Really?"

"You don't know them. They'll make life a living nightmare."

Another sip, yes, that was helping to clear his mind. "Well, I suppose you could make an excuse. Tell them the complex is doing maintenance on the apartments."

She was frowning. "I could try that, but I don't know how long it will last. They're very perceptive."

He nodded. Honestly, he really didn't feel like sorting this out after the bizarre night they'd just had. "Yep, that is an issue. But you can't stay here Cara, Caroline." He corrected himself. That nickname was becoming more comfortable to him. He took another sip of coffee, definitely helping. "And there is the other issue," her green eyes widened slightly. "The woman,"

"Oh, you mean the red-haired woman." She was sipping her own coffee. But he could tell clearly by her expression that she'd thought he was referring to that other matter of a late-night kiss, but not just yet for that topic. There were so many things to be settled.

"So, I'd like you to pack up and head to your mother's house before I leave. I don't want you here alone."

She sighed deeply, "I hate that they're driving me out of my apartment."

"Well, we've made great strides here. Just be a bit patient."

"And how in the world will we find this woman?"

He eyed her calmly, "Don't worry about that. I have a few ideas."

♦

Before they parted ways, she to Prytania Street and Max back to Magazine Street, he followed her over to City Park where they'd agreed to have some beignets at the Morning Call and decompress after their eventful night. As things had begun to sink in, Caroline couldn't help but feel more than a bit depressed and completely exhausted.

It weighed on her at times that she didn't have a less complicated life. Instead of ordinary problems, she had to deal with psychic attacks and walking around feeling completely drained of energy. Then again, her mother and Aunt Elise had told her long ago that everyone had to deal with complications from a more spiritual plane. Just because people went through life not recognizing this didn't mean it wasn't happening. And their refusal to acknowledge the spiritual component of life actually made them more vulnerable in many ways.

"We are not just bodies," Aunt Elise had told her on more than one occasion. "What we do affects our soul and spirit. No choice is without consequence."

But she had to wonder what choice she'd made that she was now feeling the effects of. Or perhaps she was just feeling the effects of someone else's choice. But what confounded her greatly was that she knew one of the central Wiccan beliefs. It was that whatever you do to someone else returns to you threefold. So, whatever this red-haired woman and Delia were practicing couldn't be true Wiccan. Clearly, it was a dark aberration, but this didn't comfort her, not one bit.

She and Max sat rather silently at the black wrought iron table outside the Morning Call, quietly eating beignets and attempting not to get powdered sugar painted all over themselves. She glanced up at Max and couldn't help but smile a bit. He was usually so dignified, but, at the moment, a dusting of white sugar was clinging to his mustache. He looked up at her as though reading her thoughts which, in retrospect, he very well could be doing. "Is it that bad? This place is often my undoing."

"I've seen worse. So, you come here often?"

"Well, not here. Chloe and I used to frequent the Café Du Monde in the French Quarter."

She nodded, sipping a café au lait that was much better than the coffee she'd made this morning. "You must miss her."

He glanced up. Seeming a little surprised, she thought that she was comfortable exploring this. As it was, she'd always been taught to speak her mind and tackle things head-on. "Yes, I do. I think more so as time goes in companionship. We were good friends."

"Yes, being friends is so important. I would think." She commented quietly, feeling, well, more than a bit lost. And then she felt his hand on hers. "You know, it will be all right."

I hope so. I really do."

◆

Caroline, more than anything in the world, wanted to sleep. She wanted to curl up in her white, wrought iron daybed that she'd slept in since childhood in her old room with its bench by the window built directly into the wall. All of this was so comforting. Although her mother had changed it a bit since she'd left, converting it into a guest room, it did still feel like hers. She desperately wanted to burrow into its safety, but to do that she had to placate the lioness who wasn't buying any of her fabrications.

Cassie Breslin had perched herself on the window seat in Caroline's haven. And, as it was, it didn't look like she intended to budge any time soon.

"So, you say they're renovating at your apartment complex?"

"Yes," she said, smiling but looking longingly at the bed beckoning her with its comfort. It was true they hadn't gotten much sleep last night. That particular fact hadn't begun to slam home until just now.

"And they're working today?"

"Yes, Mom." She was sitting just on the edge of the bed, feeling her eyelids wanting to drift down.

"On a Sunday?" Caroline's eyes snapped open.

"Uhh, yeah, seemed kind of weird to me as well. But you know the noise is very distracting. Do you not want me to stay here?"

Cassie's eyes hardened a tad. "Of course I do, darling, but they didn't give you any notice that they would be doing this work?"

"Um, no, I mean I may have missed it. I don't always read all my mail."

"Do you think that's very prudent? You might miss something important."

She nodded in agreement. Her head had begun to pound at the relentless inquisition. "Yes, you're right of course." She put on the sweetest expression that she could muster. "I've certainly learned my lesson."

Again, it seemed to go unacknowledged. "So, what does Max think of all of this?"

"Max?"

"Yes, does he think it's a good idea that you stay here now?"

Her eyes widened a bit. "Um, I don't know." She was in dangerous territory now. She could feel it all over her skin.

"You told him, didn't you?"

"Well, yeah, I think I mentioned it."

"So, you're seeing a lot of him then?"

She frowned, "You know we haven't known each other that long."

Cassie continued to eye her as though she was systematically pinning down her prey. "You know, your Aunt Elise says that you two look as though you've known each other for much longer."

Now she was getting irritated. This certainly felt intrusive, and she wanted to go to sleep. "Look, Mom, if you want to know something, just ask. If not, I'd like to take a nap. I feel like hell."

"Are you sick?"

"No, tired. I didn't sleep well last night."

"Well, I'm sorry about that, Cara." But she didn't move, not an inch.

"And?" Caroline prodded with aggravation.

"I like him, Max Gravier. He seems attentive to you."

"Yes, he's a very nice man."

"Are you two dating now?"

Caroline stared at her, a bit dumbfounded. It was just like her mom directly addressing the pink elephant standing in the middle of the room.

"I, no, we're friends, getting to know each other."

Cassie's expression softened a bit. "But you'd like to, wouldn't you?"

Caroline just stared at her. She hadn't stopped to think, really think amid this chaos, what she would like or want. "Honestly, I don't know right now."

And on this Cassie stood up, somehow satisfied, although Caroline couldn't fathom in what respect. "Okay, well then, get some rest," then she headed to the door.

"Mom," she said, and Cassie hesitated, momentarily turning back. "Thanks."

And there was a smile that told Caroline she'd indeed been granted a reprieve, even for just a little while.

PETER NORFLEET

17

Max was tired today but focused, completely focused. Once he got home, he showered and then took some time for a meditation. Not the kind that he and Caroline had embarked on, but one wholly devoted to recharging. He concentrated on clearing out the residue of negative energy that he'd encountered these last few days – the creature in Caroline's bedroom, the scarf incident, and, lastly, the attack upon Caroline last night. All of it had been incredibly draining and had left its mark.

So, he focused on achieving a higher energy vibration that would simply repel all the negative energy that seemed to be trying its best to cling to him. He thought of Caroline. This was something that he needed to teach her. He would have if she'd been here with him.

He thought to call her but felt she needed some time. Hopefully, time to rest, spend with her family, recharge in her way, and perhaps even time to think.

When he'd finished this meditation, it was just after twelve, just a little while before he opened the shop.

It was a battle despite his good intentions. He really wanted to call Caroline, just to see how she was. He knew, however, that the best way to help her was to settle this matter and end these attacks. So instead, he phoned Peter Norfleet.

Peter was someone that he'd met not long after he'd first opened Gravier's Bookshop. He wasn't a psychic. He was a PI, once a detective for the New Orleans homicide division of their police force. He went private, but as it happened, and to Max's good fortune, he was also an avid reader. He was quite the history buff of the old city, and on occasion, Max had encouraged him to publish himself, so expansive was his knowledge. But he didn't, and after Chloe died, they had spent more than a few nights grabbing a late-night beer or dinner down in the quarter.

Peter was a bit older than Max, early fifties, and divorced with two kids. He was a pragmatic fellow that didn't have the psychic sensitivities that Max possessed, but he did have re-markable instincts and an open mind—and as it was, he owed Max a favor. More than once over these past several years, Max had aided him on cases. Once, he used his particular skills to find a kidnapped girl, and another time located a body. So, knowing he needed to find someone made him think immediately of Peter.

"Peter."

"Ah, Max, calling on a Sunday, business or pleasure?"

"I need to find someone."

There was a pause, and then a moment later, "Yeah, well, let me fire up my computer and then give me all you have."

◆

Caroline dreamed of walking in a cemetery. This time she knew without question that she was dreaming, but it made her uncomfortable, nonetheless.

She knew the cemetery. It was a smaller one uptown, right in the center of the garden district. She tried to will herself to awaken, but something prevented her, not in a bad way, but in a softly obliging way. *Just follow*, it whispered.

It felt cool, and a breeze rustled through her long skirt—a long silky skirt and sandals, not unusual garb for her to wear. The tall trees shifted, and she looked up just in time to see a white bird propel itself out of their limbs. Fluidly, it stretched its great wings and began to soar overhead.

"Yes, this one is lovely." She could hear a distant voice.

And in her mind, the heron flying above her was shockingly captured, sealed in the frame of a picture. *Follow*, again, a voice.

In another moment, she was standing outside the cemetery somewhere, staring across the street at some sort of business that looked as though it used to be a wood frame house. All around it, like an envelope, was an aura of pulsating red.

She awoke to the sound of her cell phone ringing. Her eyes focused on the small clock on the bedside table that read two. She'd been asleep for a while. She picked up the phone, answering groggily. "Yes."

"Caroline."

"Max," she said, trying to rub her eyes out of disorientation.

"Were you asleep?" he asked.

"Yes, it's okay. What's wrong?"

"I just wanted to let you know that I might have tracked our mysterious redhead."

"Really?"

"Yes, I fed what I knew to a friend, and he came up with a name. A Louise Bassett, she owns a small art gallery."

"In the garden district," she murmured.

"Yes," he said quietly, not inquiring how she knew this. "It just so happens she's hosting a special showing there tonight. How would you like to attend?"

She took a deep breath, trying to steady herself. "How dressy?"

◆

Max was picking her up at seven to take her to an art show at a small art gallery owned by possibly their mysterious redhead. Louise Bassett could be the same woman that could be behind the psychic attacks on her. She wished fervently that instead, they were going to dinner and a movie. Evidently, you had to buy tickets to the event, which was exactly what Max had done. But what was concerning her most pressingly, at the moment, was that she hadn't packed clothing for such an occasion, just for work the next day.

So, Caroline was doing the only thing she could, pilfering her mother's closet. She did find, however, what Cassie and evidently Coco Chanel had termed to be an absolute necessity for any wardrobe, an LBD—aka little black dress. And strangely enough, although from more than a few years back, it worked perfectly — fitted, coming to just below the knee, with a halter top. Well, honestly, when did you ever see a halter top these days? But it was striking, and she wondered distractedly, looking at her image in the long oval, brass mirror tucked in the corner of this guest room, if Max would think so. After all, minus the demented psychic attacker that they were tracking, this was sort of like a date.

She frowned at her image, although she had to admit she looked fetching. This was nothing like a date.

A light knock at the door pulled her out of her disturbing contemplations. "Come in," she answered.

Her mother walked in smiling, flanked closely by her aunt. "Look who dropped in. How did the dress work out?"

Caroline stepped out from the corner of the room. "I think fine. What do you think?"

Cassie eyed her up and down, still smiling, while Aunt Elise was expressionless except for one tell-tale eyebrow raising. "Perfect, except I have a silky black shawl you might want to wear as a cover-up."

"Yes, do cover up," Elise murmured.

"Now come on. She looks lovely, very elegant."

Elise settled on the bed, her eyes continuing to canvas Caroline in a way that made her quite nervous. "So, he's taking you to an art show?"

"Yes, a gallery not far from here, off Washington Street."

Cassie's smile broadened just a tad. "Kind of sudden, I thought you weren't feeling well. You practically slept through lunch."

"Well," she said slowly, "I'm doing better."

Again, her aunt's steely green eyes were on her. "And your mother tells me you can't stay in your apartment now, something about renovations on Sunday."

"Yes," she answered a bit crisply.

Again, smiling at her, Cassie prodded. "Honey, we're just a bit worried about you. Things, well, they don't seem to be adding up."

Elise grimaced, "None of this is holding water, Cara."

Her eyes widened a bit. Of course, she remembered this from her teenage years after her dad had died — their Good Cop/Bad Cop shtick. Lovely, this was all she needed now.

Best to take the offensive and hope they backed off. Putting her hands on her hips, she hoped she looked formidable enough in her mother's LBD. "So, what are you saying that I'm lying?"

Cassie's brilliant smile dimmed just a notch. "No, of course not, dear."

And Elise chimed in right on her heels, "Yes, we think you're lying."

"Elise, please, that's not exactly the case."

Again, with the Mr. Spockish eyebrow, "Best not to beat around the bush. None of this makes sense. As doesn't your quick mix relationship with this bookstore fellow. It's time you tell us what's really going on."

Caroline was exasperated and so tired. She looked from one to the other, her aunt's steely face and her mother's wide-eyed expression, concerned but strangely hopeful. "All right," she began, knowing they were far too sensitive to let this go. "You're right. More is going on. But I'm trying to handle it."

"With Max?" Cassie asked.

She sighed audibly, "Yes, he's helping me."

"And you're sure he's the right person to help you?" her mother queried with great trepidation.

"Yes," she replied, "I do."

And then Cassie was on her feet, suddenly taking Caroline's hands. "And will you promise me that if you get in over your head, you'll let us help you?" Those wide blue, comforting eyes she remembered from childhood.

"Of course, Mom," she answered.

Then Cassie nodded, "Okay, Elise, let our girl finish getting ready."

Elise looked a bit confused. "That's it?"

And then Cassie smiled with genuine warmth. "Yes, Caroline can handle herself."

THE WHITE HERON

18

Did he have a plan? He grimaced, not completely. This was a reconnaissance mission, exploratory. But Louise Bassett would of course, know Caroline and, if she was highly aware, perhaps him. He wanted this confrontation. He hoped it might frighten her enough that she'd run for the hills. At least, that was his hope. He knew without question that he must keep his wits about him, but Caroline looking so amazingly beautiful tonight wasn't helping to keep his mind focused.

"Okay?" he asked Caroline, sitting silently beside him in the car since he'd picked her up not five minutes before. He was greeted at the door with what he could only describe as trepidation. Cassandra Breslin was friendly but nervous, and the aunt was downright icy, blanketing him with a cold stare of disapproval.

"How did you find her again?" Caroline asked quietly.

"Oh, an old friend of mine is a PI. We have a particular way of working. He asks questions, and I tell him what I sense until he narrows down a perpetrator."

"A perpetrator?"

"Yes, that's what he usually calls it. And in a sense, I suppose Louise Bassett fits that description. In any case, the more he questioned me, the more I had a sense of where she lived, where she worked, what her surroundings felt like, and we narrowed it down to this gallery—*The White Heron*."

"You're kidding. Is it called *The White Heron*? I was dreaming about that earlier. I mean a white heron flying overhead."

He didn't show much reaction to the news, not seeming too surprised, but then considering how they both lived. "Well, I guess we're getting help from more than one source. And before we get there, I was wondering what exactly you told your mother and your aunt. I could detect a particularly artic atmosphere when I arrived."

"Oh, well, first I lied, and then I told the truth. But not much, just that something was happening, and we were handling it."

He sighed, knowing that learning just that little bit must have driven them crazy, "I see."

"And are we? Handling it, Max?"

He turned down Washington Street, heading down several blocks toward the gallery. "Well, we're getting there."

Caroline took a deep breath and felt all the upset and weariness of the past few days simply crashing down on her. She was in no shape to do battle. At times, she felt like she was in no shape to draw the next breath. It was true that she was ready, simply ready to put up her white flag and crawl into a hole somewhere in defeat.

She placed her hand on Max's wrist and said slowly and deliberately. "I'm sorry. I thought I could do this, but I don't think I can."

She felt the car slow, and then she saw him smoothly turn into an empty parking lot in front of a darkened row of brick buildings. It looked to be shops and offices at a strip mall. She'd removed her hand but didn't look at him, didn't look at him as he turned off the car.

"Cara," it shook her. He was using that name that only her aunt and her mother ever used, only the people who really loved her.

"I'm sorry," she whispered. "It's just hit me terribly, the feeling that I can't go on. I can't do one more thing. It's too much, and I'm so tired."

He'd grabbed her hand, but she still didn't look at him. She didn't want to be this way, didn't want to seem weak to him. "You can't let her win. You can't let someone else do this to you."

She took another breath, but it felt odd, like she couldn't get enough. She couldn't quite reach that aching part of her lungs that needed to be filled. "You don't understand. My life has always been this way. My mother took great pains to protect me. Being the way I am, she knew the world would be difficult for me. But I wanted to prove them wrong, to strike out on my own, and now all of this. It just proves they were right. It proves I belong in some cocoon somewhere."

He squeezed her hand. "No, you're wrong. You're special, spectacularly unique, and you mustn't allow anyone to use you as a shortcut for what they want."

"I'm just," she didn't want to cry again, but it seemed to be happening. "I'm so tired."

"That's because someone is draining your energy. They feel they have the right to just take because they've found some ugly insidious way to do it. But they don't."

She turned to him, finally. He was staring at her with concern but something else, steely determination. "How can you be so strong in this?" she asked, amazed at the rock of support he had continuously been for her.

"Because you've given me something I haven't had in so long, maybe never, something to fight for."

Then he leaned over in the car, pulling her toward him, and kissing her, then kissing her again. And she felt his energy and his strength pouring right into her.

◆

It was a house, a wood frame house with a short spray of steps ascending to a porch that wrapped from one side across the front and down the other side. There was a small lot on its left, but as was the case often in New Orleans, it was predominantly street parking. The house itself, or should she say instead the gallery, was quaint, charming, painted a light blue with large picture windows in front and a rustic wooden sign hanging from the front porch that read *The White Heron*.

Night had already mostly descended, but streetlamps illuminated the place, ample interior lights as well as some on the porch, and oddly enough, strings of Christmas lights wrapped around its front wooden posts. Warm, cozy, and wretched, Caroline couldn't help but think, standing in the darkened side parking lot, staring morosely at the building. It was busy—well-dressed people milling around on the porch, in and out of the open door at the entrance. It looked correct, inviting, but something was terribly off. It was not unlike the start of a Stephen King novel, beginning in a lovely small town with something horrible percolating just beneath the surface.

Beside her, Max linked his hand in hers. "Are you all right?" he whispered.

"I hate this place. It feels hellish."

"Picked that up, did you?" he commented dryly.

She felt stronger with him next to her. She felt stronger with his arms around her, kissing her with abandon. But they were here for a purpose. "Do I look all right?"

"You look like you've been madly making out with some lucky bloke."

She turned to him with a bit of a grin that she couldn't suppress. "Really?"

"No, you look lovely. I just wish we had the evening to ourselves. So, shall we?" he indicated with one hand pointing a bit toward the gallery.

She nodded, "I suppose." But truthfully, she would have preferred to be almost anywhere else in the world.

Showdown

19

The air was filled with a strange sort of rose petal incense that he found more than a bit stuffy, irritating his nostrils. Then again, he'd never been one for scents, potpourri, incense, strong perfume—none of it. Fortunately for him, Chloe had indulged him in that regard, although she had been fond of the stuff.

There was some strange New Ageish string music playing in the background as people milled from room to room in the small house filled to the brim with its decorations and exhibits. He and Caroline had signed in at a small counter in the first room administered by a young girl, younger than Caroline, no more than earl twenties, he surmised—a thin, slight redhead with short hair and large brown eyes. She didn't feel good to him at all — not a bad person but one who was weak. Perhaps she had rubbed elbows with dangerous people one too many times. And, of course, unmistakably, there was a slight resemblance to the other redhead who had yet to make an appearance.

Caroline was still holding his hand as they drifted away from the counter. She seemed to be clinging to him a bit which he had no issue with. In fact, he really liked it. Outside of the situation's bizarreness, they felt like a couple. He couldn't help but wonder, once this was over, what exactly would remain of this feeling. Admittedly, he was anxious to find out.

"Did you see that girl? The young one behind—"

"Yes."

"Something is really off there."

Other customers moved past them. They smiled and nodded but said little. It was hard for him to get a fix on much of anything. It was so crowded, so packed with varying energies, that felt largely bad at the moment. They crossed the threshold into another room filled with paintings on its walls and various tables of crafted ornaments. As he began to drift inward, he entertained the thought that this would be a total wash.

But then he felt Caroline stop short beside him. She just stood there, rooted to the spot. And then he followed her gaze to the other side of the room. Her attention was fixed on a group of people huddled in the corner, laughing and referring to various bird paintings. Next to him, Caroline squeezed his hand strongly.

Almost in the next beat, and he mused afterward, perhaps in response to their presence, a short woman amidst the group dressed in a bright, coral-colored dress and brocade floral shawl spun around in their direction. Of course, he knew her immediately from the vision with Delia and from the attack on Caroline.

And it was more than clear that she knew them because almost instantly the complexion of her face seemed to blanch a few shades whiter.

◆

"You always have to be aware, Cara. The world is filled with all sorts of people. Some are true-hearted, and some are natural born thieves, thinking they can gain power through cunning and cheating."

She'd been a teenager when they'd had this conversation, but it had stuck with her. "So, you've met people like this?" she'd asked because she'd been a teenager who didn't want vague counsel but rather nitty-gritty details for her imagination to devour.

Aunt Elise had frowned as though her focus was not here with her on her mother's back patio but instead caught up far away in some distasteful memory. "Yes, unfortunately, more than a few. Now, you being a sensitive will make you more vulnerable. There will be people who will covet what you have, ache for the power they perceive. Not at all be able to comprehend the burdens that such gifts bring. And not realizing at all that to try to take, to steal away another's gifts, only leaves you with emptiness."

"Is that really true?" she asked, not wholly accepting that to take something left you with nothing.

And then her aunt had focused on her with her dark green eyes. "Well, of course, it is. I said it, didn't I?"

She zeroed in on the figure of Louise Bassett standing silently amidst a crowd of art enthusiasts. And there were things Caroline knew immediately without needing to be told.

The woman had an ego.

She wasn't nearly as formidable as she'd like everyone to think.

She was drunk with her own perceived power.

And she was shocked down to the tips of her scrunchy little toes that Caroline and Max were standing in the middle of her pseudo-art gallery.

In addition, she hadn't spoken a word.

"Louise, are you well?" a tall gaunt, brunette woman on her side.

"Do you need something, darlin?" a short, balding, walrus-mustached man flanking the other hip.

Beside her, Max squeezed her arm.

But Caroline continued to stare at her, stare into her overly eye shadowed, slightly bloodshot eyes. She could look away, but she didn't want to. She was feeling too much, how she'd lured Delia, poor pathetic, needy Delia, into her web. But Delia had become a shell, used and drained easily of energy, so instead, she used her as a tool to reach a bigger fish—to reach Caroline.

Max nudged her sharply, and finally, she pulled her attention from the tarantula to him. He was holding a strange little ceramic bowl that was less attractive than something she might pick up at the grocery. "You know," he said, a bit too loudly. "I think I'm going to buy this. Couldn't you use this on your coffee table?"

She looked at him in confusion and then noted something in his eyes. And it made her think about the scarf and the things Delia had taken from her. "Yes," she said slowly. Her eyes returned to Louise Bassett, who was now staring directly at the ceramic bowl with a fearful expression. Such a simple thing, but battles were often won with a million little things.

Max had hooked his arm in hers, pulling her back towards the other room. "Come on. I think we're done here," he murmured.

"That's it?" she asked as they approached the sales counter. "No lightsaber battle?"

He laughed softly. "Maybe next time."

A Family Meeting

20

But that wasn't quite it. And she really hadn't believed it would be so simple. "Why didn't we talk to her, confront her, beat the crap out of her?"

"It wouldn't have worked."

"She's a little bitty woman. I'm sure we could have taken her." She laughed, perhaps a bit too cheerfully.

He was tapping the car wheel, trying, she thought, perhaps to block out her rambling so that he could think. "Yes, as satisfying as that might have been for you, all it would have accomplished is getting us thrown into jail. We bought the dish and let her know in no uncertain terms that she is exposed."

Her head was aching a bit, although admittedly, for some reason, locking eyes with the old bitch did seem to have helped her. "Okay, the significance of the ugly dish?"

"We're building a defense."

"Oh, okay, what's next?"

"Call your mother and tell her you've decided to spend the night at your apartment."

"Are you kidding me after the last interrogation debacle?"

"We'll head there so you can pick up your things."

"Okay, why exactly? Why is this, Max?"

"Because tonight we go to battle."

◆

"I know it's confusing, but I decided to spend the night there. It's just easier for me to get ready for work."

Cassie was glaring at her. God, she didn't need this. Things were bizarre enough. "And you need Max to escort you home?"

She zipped her small overnight bag. "He's being gallant."

"Look, Caroline. I know you are taking pains to exclude me from whatever is happening, but do you think rushing into an involvement with this man is wise?"

She turned around and sat on the bed feeling a bit as though the wind was knocked out of her. "Involvement?"

"You're spending the night together, aren't you?"

"What? No." At least she didn't think they were, at least not in the way her mother suggested.

"I realize you are a grown woman with the right to make your own decisions."

"YES." She stated flatly.

"But these things are complicated. You know that. There are no casual involvements, not in terms of energy of spirit. They can be quite complicated and, at times, quite damaging."

"Mom, I know all of this. You don't have to worry."

Cassie crossed her arms in front of her. "I am worried. I'm terrified for you. I can feel it, just not put my finger on it."

It was clear her mother was upset. She could sense it all over her. So instinctively, Caroline stood up and hugged Cassie, tightly wrapping her arms around her. "It's all right, Mom," she whispered.

Then the unexpected happened. She felt Cassandra absolutely stiffen in her arms and take a step back. Almost a frozen look had dropped across her features. "Who is this woman? This Louise Bassett?" Caroline's heart sank. The contact had done it. She'd seen too much. "What in the hell are you two doing?"

"Mom."

"You're leaving here over my dead body," she said with icy fear in her voice.

Caroline's head was reeling. This was too much on top of everything else. So, she did the only thing she could think of. "All right, let's go downstairs and talk to Max. We'll explain everything."

♦

Cassandra Breslin's favorite room was a small sunroom/library with a rounded wall on one side in conjunction with the Queen Anne turret curve on the outside of the house. It wasn't an enormous room. In the morning, the sun flooded inward, warming the furniture, and sometimes in the evening, she swore the moonlight bounced off the windowpanes. It was a place of retreat for Cassie, but just at this moment, it was crammed full of people.

Elise hadn't left yet that evening. Instead, she had been holed up in Jared's room, helping coach him through a trigonometry class he was taking in college. So, Cassie had summoned them both, and with Caroline and Max Gravier, her little quiet retreat was very packed. The window seat along the curved wall held Caroline, Jared, and Elise while Max stood next to them as Cassie paced the small circular space.

"Why was it necessary to keep this all a secret, Caroline? This is all very serious."

"Caroline's not a kid, Mom. She wanted to handle this alone," Jared piped up. Cassie looked crossly at him. She expected him to take her side on this, but admittedly, he was always a wild card.

"This woman is not a Wiccan," Elise grumbled, more than a bit out of sorts. "If she practices any faith, it is not Wiccan in any shape or form."

"Well, as Max said, we're planning on settling this tonight, building a protection," Caroline rambled on. It was clear that she felt more than a bit on the defensive.

She looked up to Max for confirmation, but he was silent. He'd talked a bit earlier, explaining what had been going on and what he hoped to accomplish, but now seemed oddly quiet. Then again, Caroline felt he was doing so deliberately, giving her family a chance to voice their opinions.

Again, Cassie crossed the small space that was her retreat. "I don't like it. I don't like Cara so vulnerable in all of this. I would like to handle this without her."

"That's not fair to Cara," Elise spoke softly, but what she said greatly surprised Cassie, who now was feeling unexpectedly outnumbered.

She zeroed in on her younger sibling. "You don't think I'm being fair to Cara?"

Elise frowned a bit, then spoke sternly but calmly. "As Jared said, she is a grown woman, and her life will come with these challenges. The plan Mr. Gravier laid out is sound. I know you are afraid for her as I am, but she must make her choices. If she needs us, she will tell us."

Caroline was staring at her Aunt Elise in a bit of shock. She certainly hadn't counted on her support in this. "Yes, of course, I will."

"And Cassie and I will concentrate our energy to support your endeavor this evening, Jared as well."

Jared straightened up, looking a bit surprised. "Yeah, sure."

Cassie looked at all of them and their faces, knowing they were right. But she also seemed unable to shed the dread that had wrapped around her heart. "Well then, Max," she enunciated rather deliberately. "I am placing my daughter in your hands. Please see that no harm comes to her." And then she turned and walked out of the room, leaving them all a bit speechless.

◆

She stared outside her bedroom window that overlooked the street below, watching as Caroline's car drove away, followed closely by that of Max Gravier. She wasn't a cold woman. She had hugged her daughter goodbye, wishing them luck and pledging her support. But her heart wasn't in it. She glanced around the bedroom. She had shared this room for so many years with her husband. It wasn't exactly what one would call a loveless marriage but not exactly a loving one either. Her husband had seen what he wanted to see and lived in the world that he preferred to live in. Not too deep, not too complicated, and simply did not acknowledge the rest. Unfortunately for her, she was often part of that other world that he did not want to see. And as a result, he often didn't "see" her at all.

She drew a breath feeling pain from that obscure spot in her heart that never seemed to heal. She certainly didn't want that sort of life for any of her children. She wanted them to be fully loved and appreciated for who they were, not for who someone else wished them to be.

She sat on the edge of the queen-sized bed she had bought after her husband died, replacing the one they had used together and much of the furniture in the bedroom. She had desperately wanted to start fresh. But had it worked, or had she just cocooned herself in this house that had never fully felt like hers?

Elise drifted into the room, lingering somewhere near the door. "Dark thoughts, my sister?" she murmured.

"The darkest," Cassie responded. "I can't shake it, a feeling of foreboding."

"Well, pull yourself together. I have Jared setting out white candles in your little turret room. We'll work from there."

She turned to her sister in a bit of confusion. "You mean to send energy."

She smiled, "Well, that's just the beginning. We're team two."

"Team two?" she questioned.

"Yes, we're traveling tonight."

THE ASHFORD GIRLS

21

They were only a few blocks from her apartment when Caroline realized she was still wearing her mother's dress. The whole sequence of events had happened so quickly that she'd forgotten she still had it on.

She desperately needed to calm down, or she would literally be capable of doing nothing. The downside of being so empathic or sensitive, as the psychics liked to term it, was that one tended to be a pleaser. When you could FEEL other people's feelings with a capital F, it was wildly apparent when they were unhappy, unhappy with you, with themselves, angry or upset. Unfortunately, the negative emotions came screaming in, while the positive ones tended to be drowned out in the immediate uproar.

In any case, she realized, maybe a bit too late, that her mother's dress was bleeding its energy into her. Caroline had always been aware that her mom had been unhappy in her marriage. For some reason, perhaps involving an event that had occurred while she was wearing it, this dress held a profound amount of that sad energy. Now at the eleventh hour, Caroline realized that it had contributed in some regard to her unstable emotions that evening.

Of course, she should've realized this earlier, but too much had been happening. Suffice to say she was on extreme overload.

As she pulled up in front of her apartment and watched Max park directly behind her on the street, she knew that she needed to take off the dress and shower before they did anything else. She desperately needed to get rid of both its energy and all the negative energy that was dumped on them at *The White Heron*.

♦

On the drive over to Caroline's apartment Max had puzzled out or rather had strategized a few things. One was that they weren't quite prepared to go inside, and the second was that he needed to obtain a few items from his bookstore before they began.

Caroline, and rightly so, seemed confused when he told her that she couldn't go into the apartment yet. She seemed anxious to change. But fortunately, there was a change of clothes in the bag she'd brought from her mother's house. "I don't know why you couldn't tell me all this before," she murmured, a bit disgruntled.

All he could say was that he didn't know. These thoughts, or rather realizations as one might call them, came slowly.

So, they left Caroline's car, and she, and her bag, journeyed back to Gravier's Bookshop. "It's all right," he said, feeling her agitation as he sat beside her.

"It's just, well, that I really need a shower. I can still feel all that negative gunk from *The White Heron* all over my skin."

"You can shower at my place while I pull together a few things I need."

She didn't respond, simply silently looked out the window. She was trying to collect herself, he thought, which was wise.

The whole evening had been, at the very least unsettling, the confrontation with Louise Bassett at *The White Heron*, then the confrontation with Caroline's family at the Prytania Street house. Both had been disturbing in different ways. He'd felt a tremendous amount of power and ability amongst the Breslin family. And with Caroline's mother, a deep well of personal despair, which seemed to translate into a fierce protectiveness of her daughter. In some ways, he'd felt as though he shouldn't have been present at all, feeling intrusive. Oddly though, in the short time he'd known them, he felt he'd carved a bit of a spot for himself there. It was something that surely didn't make sense at all except for the fact that he was forming a deep and unexpected attachment to Caroline.

He hadn't anticipated this. After Chloe, he wasn't at all sure if he'd ever wanted to fall in love again, have that sort of relationship. It had been so painful, particularly at the end. Afterward, he'd felt like a soldier emerging scarred from a horrible defeat on the battlefield – every piece of his heart and soul shredded. Who in their right mind would want to risk themselves again in such a way that could cause such pain?

Oddly though, what was happening here didn't feel like that. It was different, a different sort of bond being forged, a new territory, so to speak, that was tantalizing and irresistible in its way. He supposed he could back away after all of this was settled. But he wasn't a man who tended to lie to himself. He liked the way he was feeling. He liked the seductive tendrils of excitement he felt pulling him closer toward Cara. It was intoxicating, and he was enjoying it immensely.

He squeezed her hand in reassurance. "Still with me?"

"I wish all this were behind us," she answered.

"It will be soon."

♦

Being in his shower felt intimate, particularly for someone as sensitive and empathic as she was. As the hot water flowed over her skin, removing any vestiges of her mother's sadness and the suffocating creepiness of *The White Heron*, her mind began to feel lighter. And she could feel Max, Max bathing in here, Max naked with water running off of his skin. Her senses spun with the imagery, with the feeling of him being so close to her. She breathed deeply in the steam and felt his warmth surround her.

She was foolish to become so attached so quickly, but she couldn't help it. He felt familiar to her, as though something about the two of them just fit. So, she stopped, stopped thinking, and let that realization simply seep in with the peace it offered.

◆

Max heard the sound of a blow dryer coming from the small bathroom off of his bedroom. He'd spent some time gathering the items that he felt would be of benefit tonight. Then afterward, he'd taken a few minutes trying to clear his mind so that all his focus would be on whatever was to come.

There would be two distinct possibilities. One was that Louise Bassett had been sufficiently rattled by their appearance at her gallery tonight and would simply cut her losses and back off. That of course would require a certain degree of intelligence, which he had not gleaned in his brief exposure to her tonight.

The second possibility was that her ego would get the best of her, and she would mount a full-out knee-jerk assault.

As it was, he hoped for the former but was preparing for the latter.

As he waited quietly in his bedroom for Caroline to come out of the bathroom fresh and clean from her shower, his strongest inclination would be to tuck her under the blankets in his bed and keep her warm, cozy, and safe tonight. Of course, that wouldn't solve the problem and would probably complicate matters between them too quickly. He didn't want to rush things. He wanted to allow them to evolve and flower naturally, enjoying and perhaps reveling in every little aspect of their growing connection. But he was human, and part of him, well—

The wooden door opened from the bathroom. She walked into the room dressed in jeans and an off-white tunic shirt with her still partially dripping long chestnut-colored hair pulled up in a ponytail. Her face was stripped of makeup, a bit pinkish from the shower's heat. And he was struck powerfully by what a natural beauty she was.

He smiled, suppressing the urge to pull her into his arms. "Feel better?" he asked softly.

She nodded, "Yes, what's next?"

"Time to set things straight."

♦

It had begun when they were teenagers, well actually even before they were teenagers. The Ashford girls loved to tell ghost stories and then, a bit later, loved to have séances. Sometimes it was at slumber parties, and sometimes it was just the two of them. Elise, the youngest, the dark-haired sister, became more of the medium. She would respond in ways the ghost or rather spirit would answer, whichever one they supposedly were contacting. The other girls in the neighborhood, all from houses at Pritchard Place, were greatly amused by Elise's performance. From time to time, even her voice would change its timber, deepen if it was a man they'd contacted and lighten if it was a woman or child. It was great entertainment for the group ranging from around twelve to fifteen-year-olds.

And they even thought it amusing that Elise would feign ignorance once it was over. "I really don't remember what was said," and Cassie would cover by saying, "of course, you don't, Elise," laughing.

133

Then they stopped having séances, at least not group ones, but the two sisters continued on their own. Because Cassie was a smart girl, and she'd fully accepted that Elise's performances weren't performances at all. She was a medium, and the dead had gained a voice through her.

Cassie returned to her turret sanctuary for the second time that evening. Elise had arranged candles throughout the room as well as a few large pieces of crystal quartz that she'd pulled from the living room downstairs. As she entered, Jared was just walking in behind her with two clear bowls of water. "Where are these going Auntie E?" he asked rather jovially.

"What are we doing here?" Cassie inquired, already anticipating the answer.

Elise, who seemed very focused on the arrangement of the room, commented, "We need to clear a large space on the floor for the meditation."

"The meditation?" Cassie echoed.

Elise nodded, clearly still deeply enmeshed in her plans. Of course, this was a side of her sister that she was not unfamiliar with. They all had gifts and sensitivities, but Elise's were more flamboyant, breathtaking in their scope. Cassie's were subtler, but she'd never been jealous. No, perhaps protective, although her fiery younger sibling rarely allowed that, but also supportive. "Yes, Jared will anchor us. You and I will astrally project ourselves to go aid Caroline and Max," Elise explained.

Cassie smiled in response. Not Mr. Gravier, it was Max now. "I see," she said quietly. "What can I do?" she asked because she wasn't about to protest, given that this concerned her daughter's welfare.

TRAVELING

22

They'd walked into a heavy atmosphere inside the apartment. Max could feel a difference definitively from the last time he'd been here. Almost like a spiritual humidity, the air felt thicker. It seemed more laborious to move through it and more difficult to think clearly. It had all the hallmarks of a bombardment of negative energy and, of course, the irritation, which went hand in hand.

"I don't know. I might still need to leave here even if we get this straightened out." He could hear the aggravation in Caroline's voice, just as he could feel it on his skin.

"You need to try to be calm," he instructed. She continued to arrange white candles throughout the room, lighting them while he placed the large chunks of crystals he'd obtained from the shop.

He'd brought clear quartz for amplifying energy, smoky quartz for removing negativity, sodalite for focusing energy, and black onyx for protection. It was a varied collection of minerals that worked powerfully separately as well as with each other. Most people didn't understand or accept that psychic and or spiritual energy worked in conjunction with the physical world. Physical things could be done to heighten or accentuate one's psychic awareness and abilities, as with these pieces of stones, which served as conductors of energy.

He'd decided they would set up in the den, the heart of the apartment. "Are you ready?" he asked Caroline, who had finished lighting the candles.

She answered with resolution in her voice. "Yes, let's finish this."

◆

They broke rules, the two of them. Caroline had always been taught that when traveling astrally, there had to be an anchor — a person left behind. That was one reason she'd seldomly done it, although she had attempted it with her mother and aunt guiding her with limited success. But with Max, it was different. More than once, they'd traveled together with no adverse consequences. They seemed to complement each other in this regard. For them together, it seemed it was a natural sort of phenomenon.

She breathed deeply, allowing her mind to relax and focus simultaneously. They sat across from each other on the rug in the center of the den, hands with palms upright touching. She could feel energy flowing in the contact of his palms against hers. She'd never attempted anything quite of this sort, even when they were tracking the creature created by Delia or following the trail of the scarf/snake she'd planted. This seemed different. It was clear that wherever they were going, it was deeper.

It wasn't long before she felt movement within her body when there should have been stillness. The awareness enveloped her, which accompanied releasing oneself from the physical form.

Her eyes were closed, but she began to perceive the room around her. The furniture, the sofa, chairs, paintings on the wall, and small dinette close to the kitchen were there, but they were different. They were filled with varying colors that lived and pulsated with their own individual energy. Everything emanated energy. Even things deemed lifeless held energy from the life they once possessed. But to see it rather than know it was something quite extraordinary. She felt movement, feeling her form moving about the room.

Even the apartment walls refracted living color, changing, rippling with reaction to everything within. *"Amazing,"* she murmured outward.

"It's important we stay within this space," she heard Max whisper within her mind.

She looked down. His body remained sitting on the floor with his hands touching hers, but outside his form, she could see another impression of him. It was unlike anything she'd seen before. There was an outline of him, but all over him, encompassing him, was a wide prism of pulsating colors, amazing mutating shades of blue and green, gold and white, like a wild kaleidoscope generating patterns before her.

"You look different," she offered.

"We're in a deeper dimension. We must see what's happening here."

She felt his thoughts in her mind as though they emanated from hers. Again, she looked around the small space of her den that at times seemed to expand wildly, with the ceiling actually opening overhead and flooding into the sky, then contracting again as if pulsating to an unknown rhythm.

"Incredible," she thought, feeling almost pulled into some sort of current.

"Stay focused," he murmured in her thoughts.

She looked down. The floor, just as everything else around her, seemed to be refracting its own color. *"What are we looking for?"* she asked outward.

Then suddenly, almost as in accordance with her request, the wall of her den pushed toward them as though something was pressing against it. She felt a bit mesmerized watching it, not frightened, just fascinated. From somewhere inexplicable, she heard an odd pop. Then suddenly, the wall broke inward, not shattering but instead more of a punching through. In the next instant, quite randomly, some animal jumped through the freshly made hole into the room. It was black, covered in shadows at first, about the size of a huge predator cat. Then suddenly was mutating in form, straightening up into a tall figure, still cloaked in blackness.

"What is it?" she asked, somewhat in shock at the bizarre development.

"Apparently, what we were waiting for," was his answer.

LOUISE BASSETT

23

There was rain pouring down all around her, a violent thunderstorm, which wasn't unusual for New Orleans. The problem was, however, that she wasn't at all sure she was in New Orleans anymore. She was on a porch, a grand wooden porch that wrapped around a great house or perhaps a hotel of some sort. But she didn't know, and it didn't seem to matter.

There were chairs everywhere as well as small tables, and a selection of rocking chairs facing outward toward the landscape. The actual landscape she couldn't really see, though, because the violent rainstorm blurred it.

"This is a creation," Caroline murmured.

"No, this is a reality, one of mine."

Caroline heard the voice behind her, and with a sinking heart, she acknowledged that she was not alone. She tried to focus on Max, but then her mind felt clouded.

"It was you that I wanted to talk to, Caroline Breslin, not him. He doesn't have anything to do with this."

It was grating, irritating, the pitch and tenor of her voice, not smooth as it should be, not smooth as evil should be as it tried to sway you to do something you knew was wrong.

Louise Bassett stepped out in front of her, blocking her view of the thunderstorm, and Caroline's mind felt muddled. The short woman was dressed as she'd been in the bookstore—that bright coral-colored dress and the curious shawl that draped across her shoulders. She was a garish woman. No matter how appealing she seemed on the outside, Caroline would always perceive her that way. She had seen too much of the ugliness in her.

"Where is Max?" she asked again, trying to direct her mind to locate him.

"He's occupied. You didn't think I was going to come wholly unprepared?"

"Why don't you simply leave me alone?"

"Because you have something, my dear, that I need."

"Really?" she replied, not needing to ask. But then again, she felt as though she was stalling for time. Stalling for what exactly, she had no idea. "What's that?"

"Why power, of course."

♦

It had happened quickly, all of it accelerating. The apartment wall seemed to be punched open as though something of great force simply forced a hole into it.

He'd expected some sort of attack, but not as rapidly as it had happened. There was a shadowy animal jumping into the room, metamorphosing into a figure. Quickly, it had taken hold of Caroline, yanking her right back through the hole. By the time he'd reached the opening, it had resealed itself.

Max was stunned by the pure speed of the assault. He concentrated on Caroline, trying to will his essence to her, but it felt as though it was being blocked. He couldn't believe it. How stupid he'd been to allow this to happen.

Again, he willed himself into a deep concentration feeling an awareness begin to form. And then he heard the voices.

"Max."

"Where is she? Where is Caroline?"

Focusing deeply on their source, the figures of Cassandra Breslin and Elise Ashford began to materialize.

"How?" he began.

"No time," the now apparent figure of Elise communicated rapidly to his mind. *"Caroline?"*

"She's taken her somewhere, somewhere I can't reach."

Quickly, she turned to Cassie beside her. *"I want you to focus on your bond with your daughter. If anyone can find her, it's you."*

Elise held out her hand to Max. *"We need to all combine our strength."* And the three formed a circle. As they did immediately, he felt a powerful surge of energy, then a shift in focus. Around them, reality swirled, and they were in another place.

"Is she here?" Cassie asked.

"Close," was Elise's reply.

◆

Caroline's head swirled with dizziness, and she felt weak. It wasn't good for her to be here, not at all. "I don't understand what you want. You have Delia."

The short redhead leaned against a massive granite column, and Caroline blinked. Wasn't this porch made of wood? But it wasn't now. It was cold, drafty stone, and the storm still raged outside. She glanced around, not homey rocking chairs but cold granite benches, clearly not a terribly stable reality.

"Delia is a child, weak, not like you and I."

"A child? I'm sure she wouldn't appreciate that description."

The already cold, dark eyes hardened, and Caroline continued to try to locate Max. How far could he be?

She felt another wave of dizziness. "You're so tired, my dear. Perhaps you should rest," she coaxed in that very stringent voice that seemed to rake painfully across her mind.

◆

There wasn't a lot of light here, but rather shadows and dark, soupy, quixotic layers of negative energy.

"What is this?" he asked, perhaps to himself.

But he felt Elise and Cassie's grasp and then an answer. *"It's a pocket of her reality. Something she has managed to create, although very small."*

He moved a bit but felt slushiness around them as though they were in some swampy sort of bog. *"Is this where Caroline is?"*

"Yes," Elise answered, *"although she has a fog across her mind. She can't see it for what it is."*

"Elise, it's so hard to hold onto her. That bitch keeps interfering."

"Be calm and focus, Cassie."

"How could she have the power to do this?" Max asked.

"If you degrade your soul enough, it can contact very negative and subhuman forces. She's tapped into that power. But she's weak. She needs the energy to maintain her links."

"Caroline?" he asked in panic.

"Stay strong, Max. Yes, she's attempting to drain her completely, to absorb her very spirit."

◆

"What are you doing to me?" Caroline asked. She was so tired. She felt like she wanted to simply sleep, to just collapse on the cold, damp granite floor of this place.

She backed away from the small garish woman. But Louise continued to approach her. "No need to fight it, my dear. You should rest."

The granite was changing, becoming dark and slimy and wet, not solid at all. She continued to back up, but her back came up against something hard and slippery, as though it was wiggling against her with living things. "No need to run, just let it be," she whispered, her ugly voice scraping across what was left of her coherence.

And Louise Bassett was there, reaching out her hand toward her, her sharp dagger-like fingernails painted that bright coral to match her dress. Caroline wanted to scream, but it was impossible.

Then it stopped. The ugly, grasping hand stopped in midair. From out of nowhere, she could see another hand wrapped around the woman's plump wrist. A strong but elegant hand with long fingers that squeezed, squeezed so tightly that Louise Bassett began to wrestle against it, groaning with pain. And then, out of the thick, mucky air, another hand, a different one, grabbed the woman's face and yanked it forcibly backward. And then, in the next second, another, a man's hand, grabbing her at the waist and forcibly pulling her away.

◆

What Max could see was horrible. The creature, the shadowy creature he'd seen in the apartment, pinning Caroline up against some indecipherable dark form. Its mouth that he'd only caught a quick glimpse of seemed to be some wide gaping orifice pressed directly against Caroline's chest. He wanted to rush toward it, pulling it off her, but Elise cautioned. *"Careful, this thing is part demon now."*

So instead, the three of them surrounded it, completely linking hands. *"Concentrate on dissolving its essence,"* their new leader instructed.

He could feel panic in Cassandra's contact, which she was clearly working hard to suppress. *"Focus your white energy on its center."*

He could feel its reaction, the thing trying to maintain its contact but wriggling violently. They were hurting it. With as much force as he could muster, he continued to pierce into its very core. Screaming in its fashion, it threw itself backward off of Caroline.

"Max get her," Elise commanded. And he did, pulling Caroline back and backward from that place to where he could protect her again.

HOME

24

When they returned to the den of her apartment, Caroline was slumped over in his arms completely unconscious. Max quickly scooped her up and laid her on the sofa. Her hands were icy, and he wondered if he should call 911, just get her to a doctor quickly.

He felt panic, cold panic, and also like a complete idiot. Why in the world did he think he could handle this? What they'd encountered, in his wildest dreams he hadn't expected.

He reached for his cell phone and started calling 911 when Caroline's eyelids suddenly started to flicker open. "Oh God," he said.

And then she focused on him. "Max," she whispered.

He couldn't believe it. He was so relieved. For a moment, he'd thought and then he pushed the horrible image aggressively from his mind. He couldn't even begin to deal with what he'd contemplated. "Are you all right?" he asked shakily.

She looked at him with a bit of confusion and murmured. "Is it over?"

All he could do was to continue to touch her hand, and brush her hair from her eyes, because he had no earthly idea what to tell her.

♦

She was pale and shaky. He could feel intently that this ordeal had taken much from her. After speaking with her mother on the phone, once again they'd decided that the best place for Caroline tonight and perhaps for a while was at the house on Prytania. So, Max drove her home in his car. It was late, approaching midnight. It was nearly inconceivable to him how much had been crammed into so few hours this evening.

Caroline was quiet, almost complacent, as though all the fight had left her, while Max himself was consumed with guilt. He didn't know how to interpret what had happened, only that he'd felt enormously ill-prepared and responsible, responsible for not protecting her as he felt he should have.

As he walked beside her carrying her bag, Cassie Breslin threw open the front door of her house meeting them halfway down the stone steps that came off of her porch and throwing her arms around Caroline.

As they entered the foyer of the house as a group, he saw Elise lingering near the foot of the grand staircase. He remembered how she'd taken charge in their astral encounter with Louise Bassett when Caroline was in such jeopardy. He knew now he'd underestimated her quite a bit, written her off as a bit of an eccentric. But clearly, there was much more here beneath the surface.

"Cassie, why don't you get Caroline settled in upstairs? I'd like to have a few words with Max," Elise said.

Caroline walked over to him quietly taking the overnight bag out of his hands, whispering quietly in his ear. "Don't leave without saying goodbye," and then she did something unexpected. She kissed him softly on the cheek and then headed up the stairs with her mother. He looked up, seeing Jared watching quietly from the landing on the second floor. He was concerned about his sister. All of them were a close family, more than that an extraordinary one.

◆

He'd followed Elise into Cassie Breslin's turret room. And as he entered, it hit him how extraordinarily exhausted he was. The whole ordeal and the emotion of it had caught up with him. He sank onto the window seat as Elise remained standing, looking at him oddly. "Are you all right?" she asked.

"Yes, I'm concerned about Caroline."

"She'll be fine. Whatever hold that woman had on her has been broken thanks largely to you."

"To me?" he asked, surprised a bit considering the rant of *mea culpas* that he had been reciting in his head after Caroline had been rescued.

"Yes, don't you see that, Max? It was you that ferreted out this problem, and largely you that enabled us to foil this attack."

"I didn't see this coming. I thought I had this thing under control, and if you two hadn't stepped in—" he muttered.

"You laid the groundwork Max, exposed Louise for what she was. Yes, you didn't sense the depth of her commitment to this, but these things are hard to call. It seems she had entangled herself with a lower being, perhaps even meshed with its substance. And what we did tonight ripped that connection apart."

"And what becomes of her now?"

Her face hardened a bit. She was an interesting set of contradictions this woman — flaky, brilliant, warm, and at times icily chilling. "Hard to say, when you make such negative choices there are always adverse consequences. It's the way of the universe. How else will we learn not to harm each other?"

He waited, understanding that he would get no further elaboration. And he couldn't find too much concern in his heart for Louise Bassett. As Elise had expressed so succinctly, she'd made her choices. "Are you sure Caroline will be all right?"

She nodded. "She needs to become stronger, so she's not so vulnerable, and I think perhaps with your help that will happen sooner rather than later. I do take it that we all will be seeing a lot more of you."

He smiled in the midst of his exhaustion, feeling a bit of an invitation mingled with a new acceptance. "Yes, yes, I believe so. Seems I have a lot to learn, and this family may just help me do that."

Elise smiled slowly, "Yes, I agree Mr. Gravier."

♦

Caroline was upstairs in her bedroom when he told her goodnight. He found her staring out the window, evidently so lost in thought that she didn't acknowledge his presence right away. But then after a moment she spoke. "It all seems a blur Max."

"Give it a little time Cara, it will come back again."

She turned around, looking at him intently as though there were a thousand things she wanted to say. "I want to thank you."

He took her hands in his, "And I want to thank you as well."

She looked at him a bit teary-eyed he thought. "So, this isn't a goodbye, is it?"

And then he stepped in a bit and softly kissed her on the lips. "No Cara, this is most definitely a beginning."

Finis

148

A Murder in the Village
And Other Mystical Tales of the Ouachita Mountains
6x9 Softcover & Hardcover 274 pages
ISBN 978-1-61342-459-9
ISBN (Hardcover) 979-8-27615-496-1

At the foothills of the Ouachita Mountains, into their ancient heart, and even perhaps into nearby unexplored dimensions, slip into a series of supernatural short stories.

A clash of shapeshifters on sacred grounds, a compromised witch desperately fleeing a witch hunter, and a ghost in search of his murderer are only a few of the tales that dot this paranormal landscape.

Take a mystical diversion that could very well land you in a realm, at the least unexpected and at the most horrifying. But what is clear is that no one, ever, will emerge as they were before.

The Alchemist's Bride
6 x 9 Softcover & Hardcover 230 pages
ISBN 978-1-61342-454-4
ISBN (Hardcover) 978-1-61342-455-1

From a young age, Emmeline Lescale has been raised as an outsider by her aunt's family on the lavish estate of Belle Coeur in Vacherie, Louisiana. Ostensibly an orphan, she is treated as an unpaid servant. But in her twenty-fifth year, with her eyes on a dismal future, something radically changes.

Her father, a renowned physician who has ignored her existence most of her life, suddenly insists that she come to live with him. And New Orleans in the 1880s seems like no place for a proper young lady, especially when her father is embroiled with a mysterious young doctor whose interests venture deeply and dangerously into the world of the supernatural.

Jack Fallon, the protege of Emmeline's father, lives a life filled with secrets. His home, deep in the French Quarter on Bienville Street, is much more than meets the eye. And before too long, he draws Emma into the crosshairs of an existence that questions the nature of reality itself.

The Broken Vow
Vol. 1 of The Clandestine Exploits of a Werewolf
6 x 9 Softcover & Hardcover 204 pages
ISBN 978-1-61342-133-8
ISBN (Hardcover) 978-1-61342-420-9

In the heart of every man, there is a history. In the heart of every monster, there is a story. In this first installment of The Clandestine Exploits of a Werewolf, Ethan Garraint is on a vendetta that begins in the heart of the Pyrenees with the fall of Montségur and leads him to the streets of New Orleans nearly five hundred years later. But the person he chases isn't really a man anymore, and Ethan has been a werewolf for almost a millennium. With the aid of a gifted seer, he is on a blood hunt that will culminate in a journey that crosses the line between heaven and earth and ends somewhere in between.

The Story of Enid
Vol. 2 of The Clandestine Exploits of a Werewolf
6 x 9 Softcover & Hardcover 254 pages
ISBN 978-1-61342-453-7
ISBN (Hardcover) 978-1-61342-456-8

What happens when your one true love reincarnates, and you just happen to be a werewolf?

Ethan Garraint is an old soul. He has been alive for hundreds of years, battling countless challenges and foes along the way— not the least of which was living through the genocide of the Cathar people at Montsegur, a society that wholly embraced him despite his lycanthropic nature. But in Volume 2 of The Clandestine Exploits of a Werewolf, he faces a dilemma that brings his past and present full circle, merging them both.

The Lady in the Blue Dress
6 x 9 Softcover & Hardcover 214 pages
ISBN 978-1-61342-600-5
ISBN (Hardcover) 978-1-61342-418-6

When she was a child, Mika Devalieur was introduced to her grandmother's most precious possession—a priceless and mysterious painting that she simply called The Lady in the Blue Dress. Upon Adele St. Clair's death, the painting is left in the care of her granddaughter with only one stipulation. Mika must hand over the family heirloom to a total stranger. Mika Devalieur desperately wants to deny her beloved grandmother's last request, but she can't. Torn between her Gran's last wishes and her desire to hold onto the Lady, she ultimately journeys to rural Virginia, where an enigmatic man shows her that this painting is only the beginning.

What quickly becomes clear is that James Clairmont knows much more about her and the Lady than he is letting on. He begins to slowly unravel a powerful supernatural connection that spans three generations of her family. Mika finds herself desperate to uncover the entire truth before she falls in love with a man filled with so many secrets—secrets about him, about her, and most especially about The Lady in the Blue Dress. (First published on Kindle Vella, episodes 1-23.)

More Books by Evelyn Klebert

Dumaine Street

6 x 9 Softcover & Hardcover 306 pages
ISBN 978-1-61342-902-0
ISBN (Hardcover) 978-1-61342-416-2

Voices in her head, catastrophic emotions, hallucinations—Rebecca Wells is more than convinced that she is losing her mind. And as a last-ditch effort, she contacts a self-professed counselor who seems convinced he can help.

Gabriel Sutton has abandoned the world of medicine to navigate a realm filled with psychic phenomena. Diagnosing Becca with extreme empathic abilities, he struggles to help her stabilize her gifts while trying desperately not to fall in love with his patient.

From the realm of vulnerability into a crusade to use their profound gifts to rescue others from peril on the other side of death, these two follow an astonishing and unpredictable path into each other's hearts.

The Tethering

A Portent of Crows
6 x 9 Softcover & Hardcover 201 pages
ISBN 978-1-61342-599-2
ISBN (Hardcover) 978-1-61342-419-3

Deborah Brandt's beloved Aunt Gena always told her that she was special, a bit different, and would have to live her life, unlike other people. Of course, this she disregarded as the ramblings of her lovely but notably eccentric aunt. Although there were the things that Aunt Gena said that seemed true—like Deborah being sensitive to energy shifts, having potentially psychic impressions, and dreaming of a spirit guide—none of it could be real. But the most ridiculous thing that her Aunt Gena told her before she died was that someone special was out there for her. She said that he was an extraordinary man who was not only her perfect match but someone who she would learn from so that they could help the world in difficult times. How ridiculous! It sounds like a fairy tale, and no such person exists.

Daniel Wren is unique. He has been raised and trained from a young age to hone his psychic gifts. He lives in a world unimagined by most. And he has been waiting for years to contact his counterpart, soulmate, if you will. But the problem is that she is painfully unaware of the type of life that he lives and the life she would be entering into if they came together.

His dilemma becomes how best to proceed. How can he win her over and move forward before outside forces take that decision away from him?

Travels into the Breach
Accounts of a Reluctant Mystic
6 x 9 Softcover & Hardcover 171 pages
ISBN 978-1-61342-323-3
ISBN (Hardcover) 978-1-61342-417-9

At first glance, his life seems quiet, serene, and even uneventful. Malachi McKellan, a 65-year-old widower and author of esoteric books, lives largely as a recluse in a house situated just off the banks of Bayou St. John in New Orleans. But unbeknownst to most, he is also a bit of a detective, a specific kind of detective whose specialty is psychic attacks. Alongside his lifelong companion and spirit guide Simon Tull, a 19th-century, 20-something English gent, Malachi battles the unseen, and is an unacknowledged hero to the most vulnerable. Most of the population have no idea what is really happening beneath the surface of the world in which they live.

In this collection of adventures, Malachi McKellan and Simon Tull wage war against the most insidious elements of the paranormal. In *The Three*, Malachi and Simon come to the aid of a young woman being victimized by a group of dark witches. An old apartment building is the scene of an unimaginable battle against monstrous forces in *The Lost Soul*. Malachi and Simon find themselves strategizing against a psychic vampire in *Obsession*, and *The Hotel* turns back time to the 1980s where Malachi confronts a demonic spirit. In *Between*, a past life is revisited as Malachi attempts to rescue a beloved sister from committing her existence to vengeance, and *The Wedding* takes a personal turn when Malachi must confront painful truths while endeavoring to protect his niece from a potentially devastating union.

Travel into the breach with a pair of paranormal warriors who choose to confront overwhelming forces on a battlefield unsuspected by most.

Gravier's Bookshop
A New Orleans Paranormal Mystery (#1)
6 x 9 Softcover & Hardcover 176 pages
ISBN 978-1-61342-288-5
ISBN (Hardcover) 978-1-61342-411-7

Max Gravier had no intention of becoming a recluse, but after his wife's death it seems his life is heading in that direction. He spends his time running Gravier's Bookshop on Magazine Street and occasionally on the quiet helps the police solve a crime with his psychic sensitivities. That is until he answers Caroline Breslin's call, a cry for help out of his dreams that draws him into a fierce battle for a young woman's soul.

In this first installment of The New Orleans Paranormal Mystery series, Caroline Breslin, an amazingly gifted empath, is determined to strike out on her own and has moved out from the protection of her family home. All is going extremely well until, of course, she comes under siege from a devastating supernatural attack. The last thing Caroline wants is to run back to her family for help, even though she is painfully in over her head.

What she really needs is a knight in shining armor—or maybe just that guy that keeps haunting her dreams.

Join them and the whole Breslin family psychic clan in this first installment of The New Orleans Paranormal Mystery Series where you'll travel into a new world just a few steps into the turbulent realm of the unseen.

The Hotel Mandolin
A New Orleans Paranormal Mystery (#2)
6 x 9 Softcover & Hardcover 146 pages
ISBN 978-1-61342-290-8
ISBN (Hardcover) 978-1-61342-412-4

Peril is wrapped up in the most enticing of disguises in *The Hotel Mandolin*, the second installment of The New Orleans Paranormal Mystery series. It's opulent, classic, and one of the most renowned hotels nestled deep in New Orleans' famous business district, but something is amiss at The Hotel Mandolin.

PI Peter Norfleet is calling out the big guns to help him investigate a recent suicide at the famous establishment—his good friend Max Gravier, a formidable psychic, and his girlfriend, Caroline Breslin, a talented empath. But none of them can seem to scratch the surface of this puzzle, no one except Cassie Breslin, Caroline's clairvoyant mother, who has somehow tapped into an unexpected connection with a tragic ghost from the turn of the century. And the more she uncovers, the more dangerous and malevolent the mystery becomes

More Books by Evelyn Klebert

The House at Pritchard Place
A New Orleans Paranormal Mystery (#3)
6 x 9 Softcover & Hardcover 138 pages
ISBN 978-1-61342-292-2
ISBN (Hardcover) 978-1-61342-413-1

Nothing is really wrong with the old Warrick House on Dante St. except that there most certainly is. Nothing is exactly wrong with its new mysterious owner except that Elise is sure that something doesn't add up. It isn't obvious, but sometimes the most dangerous things aren't.

In the third installment of The New Orleans Paranormal Mystery series, with the help of her very psychic sister and her children, the Breslin clan, Elise Ashford is about to embark on a wild rescue mission straight into another dimension that will land her squarely somewhere she doesn't expect, right back into her past. She'll land full circle; in a childhood home whose memory still haunts her to this day -- *The House at Pritchard Place.*

Treading on Borrowed Time
6 x 9 Softcover & Hardcover 223 pages
ISBN 978-1-61342-214-4
ISBN (Hardcover) 978-1-61342-436-0

For Julia Moreau, life seems complicated. Emerging from a failed marriage and managing a lifetime of diabetes, she lives alone in her childhood home where she communicates with the spirit of her Great Aunt Lilia. But Julia doesn't have a clue what complicated is until she is thrust into being the key chess piece in a match between two powerful men of extraordinary abilities on the wild hunt for a mystical creature hidden in the heart of New Orleans' French Quarter. Will Julia lose her soul to the karma of a devastating past life or her heart to the love of a man driven by dark forces? What is clear is that whichever way she turns she is *Treading on Borrowed Time*.

Sanctuary of Echoes
6 x 9 Softcover & Hardcover 371 pages
ISBN 978-1-61342-211-3
ISBN (Hardcover) 978-1-61342-409-4

Ghosts unacknowledged do not sleep.

Corey Knight has resigned herself to a quiet, reclusive life spent living out the rest of her days in her childhood home on the fringes of New Orleans' French Quarter. But the unexpected specter of her deceased father plunges her into a mad quest for a missing supernatural weapon unearthed long ago. And unfortunately, her only ally is a lost love she once betrayed.

Iain Shaw returns to New Orleans, a city he abandoned a decade before while fleeing a devastating past. Here, he is forced to confront it again in the visage of the woman he once adored - one that he is now determined to get back at any cost.

Follow them both in a wild paranormal tale of discovery and redemption as they confront and unearth the echoes of a buried and unyielding truth that once tore them irreparably apart.

A Quiet Moment
6 x 9 Softcover & Hardcover 273 pages
ISBN 978-1-61342-326-4
ISBN (Hardcover) 978-1-61342-435-3

Jacob Wyss is caught in a rut, in fact on the verge of being engulfed by it. After an excruciating and disillusioning divorce, his life as an artist in a sleepy-college town at the foot of the Appalachian Mountains has become quiet, routine, and maddening in its predictability. One wintry day, his deep restlessness drives him out in precarious conditions to a largely empty bookstore nearly devoid of another living soul, nearly.

Aimee Marston isn't like everyone else. On the surface, she lives a sedate life working as a feature writer for a small local newspaper in addition to several other editorial jobs to help make ends meet. But just beneath, her existence is largely not her own. She is a sensitive, an empathetic psychic, guided by her calling to use her gifts to help others. Unfortunately, as a result, her secretiveness has made her defensive, protective of herself, and prevented her from having much of a life.

A psychic call for help sends Aimee out on a freezing January morning where her destiny and Jacob's collide sending both their lives spiraling onto an unexpected and often disturbing track. Two lonely souls connect, not by accident, but by design. Theirs is the intersection of two spiritual paths, two lovers who must struggle to overcome the phantoms of a past life, as well as the challenges of their own inner demons to carve out an extraordinary future together.

A Ghost of a Chance
6 x 9 Softcover & Hardcover 230 pages
ISBN 978-1-61342-162-8
ISBN (Hardcover) 978-1-61342-440-7

You never know what's coming next.

Jack Brennan, an ambitious high-powered attorney, dies. But that's not the end, rather only the beginning. He finds himself constrained to an inexplicable afterlife as an earth-bound spirit trapped in an old Virginia farmhouse. His only companion is a very much living, reclusive writer of campy vampire novels. The maddening problem is that Hallie does not know he is there, nor that he is somewhat reluctantly falling in love with her.

Hallie Barkly is recovering from a painful and disillusioning divorce. Out of the ashes of her former life, she has managed to somehow forge a career and exorcise her demons by writing under the pseudonym of Sebastian Winters. Slowly, she is awakening to the fact that she is not alone.

Their lives intersect, and two unconventional lovers are brought together under insurmountable circumstances. Together they must battle an unseen force hell-bent on possessing Hallie's life and bridge death itself to make possible what cannot be—to find a chance.

Dragonflies - Journeys into the Paranormal
6 x 9 Softcover & Hardcover 176 pages
ISBN 978-1-88756-072-6
ISBN (Hardcover) 979-8-32548-418-6

In every form of creation, there is a blueprint for living, for experience, for interpretation. In flight, they can twist, turn, alter direction, pause in midair, and even fly backward. The dragonfly is the master of adaptability. They are a living prism, refracting light, and color, seemingly shifting their essence.

The lesson the dragonfly gives is that life is never what it appears to be.

In "The Wizard," as a novice practitioner of magic, Aurora Finn finds herself battling against the illusions of a powerful wizard intent on separating her from the world she knows. "The Sojourners" is a gentle story of a mother and daughter whose tenancy in an old Virginia farmhouse uncovers the trials and sorrows of its former occupants. A bookstore clerk gets an extraordinary customer on Halloween night in "Late One Night at Berstrums Books." In "The Tear," a woman coping with her fatal illness unknowingly begins a track on a mystical journey that will entirely restructure her vision of the world.

These stories follow the path of the dragonfly imbued with the momentum and energy of change, taking a winding and treacherous journey that ultimately leads to truth buried beneath perception.

Breaking Through the Pale
6 x 9 Softcover 134 pages
ISBN 978-1-88756-045-0

Journey with metaphysical author Evelyn Klebert into a collection of short stories that travel beyond the pale into the unpredictable realm of the paranormal.

In "A Grey Mourning," a disillusioned man encounters a mysterious being on the foggy streets of New Orleans. "Contact" is a tale of automatic writing, when a young artist establishes communication with a spirit guide, and the victim of a car crash unravels the true nature of her existence in "Dancing on the Threshold." The final tale is called "Isolation," in which a confused and disoriented woman finds herself in an old, quaint house where she must piece together the mystical implications surrounding her predicament.

The Witches' Own
6 x 9 Softcover & Hardcover 140 pages
ISBN 978-1-61342-058-4
ISBN (Hardcover) 978-1-61342-428-5

On the surface things seem quiet and serene in the picturesque coastal village of Kilmarnock, Virginia. But something unseen roams its lush forests as the past and present collide and the unthinkable begins to wreak its vengeance. Young Lucy Bonner is executed for witchcraft in the town's distant and brutal past. Her death triggers an unholy chain of events which grasp at the restless heart of novelist Peter McQuade, spurring him towards a quest to uncover the dark and terrifying truth.

The Left Palm
And Other Halloween Tales of the Supernatural
6 x 9 Softcover & Hardcover 122 pages
ISBN 978-1-93493-556-9
ISBN (Hardcover) 978-1-61342-442-1

Halloween is the time of year when that veil between worlds is thinned, and you can just catch a quick glimpse into the realm of the unknowable. In this collection of short stories, Evelyn Klebert takes you to a place where ordinary life splinters into the sphere of the paranormal.

The journey begins with one woman's unstoppable quest for vengeance against a supernatural creature in "Wolves" and continues in an old historical graveyard where a horrifying discovery is uncovered in "Emma Fallon." In "The Soul Shredder," a psychiatrist's unusual patient opens his eyes to a disturbing new view of reality, while in "Wildflowers," a woman strikes up a supernatural friendship with impossible implications. And in "The Left Palm," a fortuneteller in the French Quarter receives a most unexpected and terrifying customer.

White Harbor Road
And Other Tales of Paranormal Romance
6 x 9 Softcover & Hardcover 152 pages
ISBN 978-1-61342-066-9
ISBN (Hardcover) 978-1-61342-441-4

A psychic soul mate, a time traveler, a horror writer, and an enigmatic stranger take a selection of resilient, life-battered heroines to a place of paranormal healing and transformation. In this collection of short stories, *White Harbor Road* is the last stop where life's burdens and hardships evolve into something unexpected.

More Books by Evelyn Klebert

Explanations
6 x 9 Softcover 82 pages
ISBN 978-1-93493-515-6

In this, her second poetry collection, Evelyn Klebert takes us down the intricate path of a personal journey. Life with its particular struggles, pitfalls, and ultimately triumphs clearly begins to mirror a universal path, the quest for answers that we all ultimately pursue. In this reflective, esoteric collection we can all explore and seek some of life's elemental mysteries and hopefully when all is said and done emerge with some *Explanations*.

Considerations
6 x 9 Softcover 84 pages
ISBN 978-1-88756-062-7

Sometimes the struggle to understand the meaning and complexities of living comes down to a single moment of introspection or a fleeting yet meaningful reflection. This collection of poetry by Evelyn Klebert takes you down a winding path of self-discovery where the resolution may not always be absolute, but the journey is indeed unforgettable. It a wide and varied map of inspired poetry for your examination and consideration.

More Books by Evelyn Klebert

Appointment with the Unknown
The Hotel Stories
6 x 9 Softcover & Hardcover 155 pages
ISBN 978-1-61342-360-8
ISBN (Hardcover) 978-1-61342-421-6

A hotel, for most, represents a normal place, a predictable realm of commonality. One might even go as far to say a safe space, the reliable where nothing particularly unusual is expected to happen. Or is it? Dimensional traveling, spirit guides, mystical storms, and soul mates separated by time are only a few elements dotting this supernatural landscape. Drop into a collection of romantic paranormal stories where that place of commonality is only the threshold, the jumping-off point, for extraordinary adventures into the unknown.

Visit Evelyn's website at:
www.evelynklebert.com

Cornerstone Book Publishers
www.cornerstonepublishers.com

www.ingramcontent.com/pod-product-compliance
Lightning Source LLC
Chambersburg PA
CBHW020653260626
47157CB00008B/3013